A HEATHENS
NOVELLA

UNHALLOWED

SHAE RUBY

ISBN: 979-8-9860000-6-0

Cover Design by: Quirky Circe

Formatting by: Quirky Circe

Edited by: Angie Ojeda Hazen (Lunar Rose Editing Services)

To everyone who wants to be chased by a depraved fictional man,

This is for you.

PLAYLIST

Right Here – *Chase Atlantic*

Church – *Chase Atlantic*

Ascensionism – *Sleep Token*

Chokehold – *Sleep Token*

Rain – *Sleep Token*

Sleeptalk – *Dayseeker*

Granite – *Sleep Token*

Limits – *Bad Omens*

Panic Room – *Au/Ra*

Angels Like You – *Miley Cyrus*

Venenosa – *Thousand Below*

Hate Me Too – *From Ashes to New*

Funeral – *Neoni*

Devil's Playground – *The Rigs*

Glass Houses – *Bad Omens*
Writing on the Walls – *Underoath*
Chills (Dark Version) – *Mickey Valen & Joey Myron*
Psycho – *AViVA*
Runrunrun – *Dutch Melrose*
While You're At It – *Jessie Murph*
Moth To A Flame – *Swedish House Mafia & The Weekend*
Teacher's Pet – *Melanie Martinez*
Breathe Into Me – *Red*
Breaking – *Anberlin*
Nightmare – *Besomorph & RIELL*
Falling Apart – *Papa Roach*
Do I Wanna Know? – *Arctic Monkeys*
Breathing – *Yellowcard*
REDRUM – *Austin Hull*
Never Know – *Bad Omens*
See Me Fly – *Roza*
Nowhere To Go – *Bad Omens*
Mess Like Me – *Foxblood*
Tourniquet – *Evanescence*
Dark Matter – *Rivals*
Until The Day I Die – *Story of the Year*
Unity – *VRSTY*
The Beast Inside – *My Enemies & I*
Shameless – *Camila Cabello*
Silhouette – *Thrice*
Evoke – *Our Promises*
Hypnosis – *Sleep Token*
3:15 (Slowed Down + Reverb) – *Russ*
Need To Know – *Doja Cat*
Voices in My Head – *Falling in Reverse*
The Apparition – *Sleep Token*
Sugar – *Sleep Token*

TRIGGER WARNINGS

Hello reader,

I write dark stories that can be disturbing to some. My books are not for the faint of heart, and my characters, many times, are not redeemable. This book contains dark themes to include graphic sex scenes, forced marriage, consent non-consent/dubious consent, captivity, primal play, blood play, choking/breath play, degradation, ritual sacrifice, murder, sharing between main characters, cult, religious trauma, male to male sexual intercourse. I may be missing some triggers, so instead, consider this a blanket trigger warning.

I trust you know your triggers before proceeding, and always remember to take care of your mental health.

For more things Shae Ruby, visit
authorshaeruby.com

CHAPTER ONE

ANGEL

The sound of the lock disengaging snaps me out of my trance, the darkness no longer casting shadows before my eyes. I'm so used to it at this point. There's nothing down here, not even a speck of light. For all I know, I could have company, but not even the sounds of my breaths register in my brain anymore.

Light filters in when the door is opened, and my eyes scream in protest before I shut them tightly. My corneas grate against my lids, reminding me that everything about me is dry at this point. Including my heart.

What is a heart anyway?

My clothes—a long t-shirt—rustle with my movements. I should be grateful they feed me well, clothe me, and make sure I'm taken care of for the most part. I'm just lacking human contact, except for Jonah—my religion teacher. Instead, as I smell the musty basement around me, all I feel is resentment, a reminder that I'm nothing to anyone. Not anymore, at least.

Footsteps shuffle down the concrete stairs and I

tense, plastering myself against the cold wall that the mattress on the floor is against. No one—from my family—visits me down here. It's only the voices in my head that keep me entertained, egging me on. Isn't that normal anyway? Don't we need stimulation to survive? And that's what I'm doing, is it not? Surviving.

Barely.

I scrape by just fine, though. After all, I've been down here for nearly a decade. It's no wonder I've lost touch with reality. The last time someone was down here with me was a few years ago, and after *they* realized what he and I were doing, how we had found comfort in each other... well, they ripped him from me.

I guess that's not true. I'm a liar, just as they keep telling me. The last time someone was down here was yesterday, but all he does is... teach me. Because, obviously, I have to learn about *The Lord*. They want me to be educated, knowledgeable. Thankfully, they didn't neglect my high school education, but it's been several years since anyone taught me about anything other than God. Probably because there's nothing else to teach. I'm too old for it now—twenty-one, to be exact. And they won't let me go to college, clearly.

Although I've been confined to small spaces for nearly half my life, trapped like a caged animal, they won't let me be a stupid, uneducated caged animal. I believe that's how they make themselves feel less guilty about what they're doing. How lucky for me.

So yeah, the man comes and goes, the flow of him coming in and out making my head pound in protest when he turns on the lights, but the religious education is necessary to fuel my hate. Because one day, I swear I'll escape this hell. I'll find a way to make it out of here and never look back.

If hell was real, this is what it would look like.

Cramped spaces. Darkness. Boredom.

The one thing no one knows is that there's no amount of forcing me into learning about a God; there's no one I'll worship except for one person. And he's gone. Dead? I don't know. But he's been gone like the wind for years.

At first, it was a platonic love—the kind where you steal smiles from each other and hold by the pinkies. Eventually, though, it grew into more, morphing from a tiny spark that ultimately turned into a wildfire. It turned into butterfly kisses in the darkness, kissing under the covers and making our own world, shaping it with our own hands until everything else ceased to be.

Tongue, lips, teeth.

Hands, skin, souls.

We were everything the other wasn't. He was my other half, and now I'm incomplete. It was unhealthy, the way everything stopped when I was in the same vicinity as him, and trapped in a basement together for years... our feelings wouldn't fit in our chest cavities any longer. We were bursting at the seams.

Until we were discovered.

"Time to go, young lady." The voice of my teacher booms and echoes in the confined space, and I flinch when he makes it to the last step. I open my eyes and squint at the bright lights, focusing on him. "It's your lucky day."

"Where?" I ask nervously, fidgeting with my hands already, tearing at my fingernails. A habit I can't fucking break. "What do you mean?"

I look at his dirty blond hair and his brown eyes. If the Devil had a face, it would be his. Strong jaw, straight nose, killer eyes. Jonah's body is strong, built with muscles that scream years of work. He's a few years older than me, and absolutely obsessed with what he does. But he's attractive, sinful. And that's exactly why he's here. To tempt me, make me a sinner, more than they already believe I am for not caring about the word of the *Lord*. "You're leaving this place." He grins. "And that's all I will say."

I eagerly get up from the bed, my head spinning from getting up too fast, and notice he has clothes in one hand and shoes in the other. He throws them at my feet and steps back, expecting me to get dressed. Jonah doesn't turn around though. In fact, he stays looking at me eagerly, as if he wants something I can offer.

Nasty fucker.

They want to preach about purity, yet look at him, watching me in a way I would say is the opposite of pure. Or maybe it's because I've lost that already and now I'm tainted. Disgusting. Just as they keep reminding me every day of my life.

"Are you going to turn around?" I ask with a tremble in my voice that pisses me off.

You must not show fear.

You must be strong.

Shut the fuck up.

He grins, an evil glare in his eyes. "No."

But it doesn't matter, because if he's being serious and I'm finally getting out of here, well I don't care what happens from now until I'm free. Let him ogle me, do more than that for all I care, but my wings are about to spread and no one is keeping me from flying.

Thankfully, all he does is stare as I replace my clothing, but it still sends a shiver down my spine from the way his eyes are trailing up and down my body. It's like he wants to reach out and touch me with them. Fuck me with them.

Let him.

No.

The voices in my head don't stop as they try to convince me of what to do, what not to do. But I choose the last one, no longer feigning nonchalance. I want to claw his eyes out despite what I was feeling just a second ago. It's too bad I don't have a fucking knife, but I bet I could find one if I tried hard enough. Just not down here.

"I will claw your eyes out if you keep looking at me that way," I tell him with a grin, and he narrows his eyes on me. He takes a small step back, knowing I'd probably do it. No, I *would* do it.

"Just finish getting dressed, little girl," he replies condescendingly.

I make quick work of tying my shoes and stand again, waiting for further instructions. He looks pensive for a moment, and for a split second I'm scared he's changed his mind. Then again, maybe it's for the best. Where would I go? How would I survive? Where the fuck even am I? How would I get out of here?

I haven't been to the outside world since I was eleven. I haven't seen the fucking sun in that long. Do I even remember where I live? How to get around? It's probably changed a lot. The neighborhood could look entirely different at this point.

Jonah tips his chin toward the door and my legs almost buckle from the nerves. Regardless, I take deep breaths and force myself to put one foot after the other until I start walking up the stairs. When I get to the last one, though... I stop and look back. My hands shake slightly, and all the bravery I was feeling moments ago slips from my dirty fingers.

It wasn't that bad down there. Yeah, it was dark, but I was fed, clothed, and left alone. No one bothered me except for Jonah a few times a day. Even that was nice... right? I can pretend none of this happened, that he didn't tell me I could leave, and go right back to my safe sanctuary.

"Move," he growls, grabbing my arm and yanking me through the doorway.

"Wait." I lick my lips, unsuccessfully digging my heels into the hardwood floor right past the doorway. Fucking shoes with no grip. "I want to stay."

"Unfortunately for you, little girl, you don't have a choice in this one."

"But where will I go?" I raise my voice, resisting,

finding my strength again. "How can you just throw me out?"

"Throw you out?" He laughs, and the hairs on the back of my neck stand on end. "Whoever said anything about that?"

"You said I'm leaving," I reply slowly, "That you're letting me go."

His grin is malicious as he levels me with a look that scares me. "No." I shake my head in denial, more fear. He can probably smell it emanating from my pores at this point. "I said you're leaving. But no one is letting you go, Angel."

My limbs lock up at his confession, and the urge to bolt renews itself. Something is wrong here, I feel it deep in the marrow of my bones. But what exactly could it—

Jonah's fist connects with my temple, making me rear back and my ears ring, and I fall to the ground, disoriented. He quickly picks me up, shuts the door to the basement and carries me somewhere else. There are stars behind my eyelids that won't disappear whether my eyes are open or closed. It. Fucking. *Hurts*.

"Whyyyyy?" I whine.

"Shut up, girl," he growls. "You need to unlearn how to speak, because the people who you're going with won't put up with your shit."

I struggle more, flailing my limbs every which way to try to get free. My attempts are futile though. "Let me go!" I scream, hoping someone will come to my rescue. But who am I kidding? Everyone hates me here. That's why

I've been trapped in my foster parents' basement. Because I have refused to become religious like them, refused to be passionate about God like them. I'm the ugly duckling, the odd one out. Always have been. Apparently, I was too much of a bad influence to stick around my siblings. Not to mention, my adoptive mother and father feel no love for me. They couldn't be bothered with me.

I'm nothing.

No one.

Disrespectful, they've called me.

A whore.

"You will learn soon that living in this basement was a mercy." He chuckles, his body vibrating against mine. It makes me sick, as bile rises to the back of my throat. "And I promise you will miss it."

"The fuck I will." But I know deep down, it's possible.

"I knew you had a mouth on you." I glare at him in disgust, but he doesn't even look at me as he walks through the house and to the front door. "But it won't serve you now."

Jonah turns the knob and pushes the front door open, making the sunlight shine right on my face. I immediately close my eyes, more like slamming them shut, scrunching them. It hurts worse than the punch to the face, and that's saying something. Heat builds behind my closed lids, a burn unlike anything I've ever felt before, and I can't tell if it's from the sun or unshed tears. Or both.

Where am I going? Why is he taking me outside?

Is someone meeting him here?

Footsteps sound closer to us, not Jonah's since he's standing still now, and my lower lip trembles. What did he get me into? Where am I going? *Where?*

"Hold her tight," a man says, and Jonah grips me harder. "*Now.*"

Jonah grabs my face with an iron grip, and the fight comes back to me. My hands reach for his face just as I force my eyes open. I'm seeing blurry and my aim is all wrong, but I manage to find his eyes and scratch. Blood immediately bubbles up, and my eyes begin to adjust. I flail in his arms and they give way, almost dropping me. I claw at him again—just as I promised —and I land on my back, a wail coming from deep within his throat and a moan coming from mine. The light is still too bright, but I manage to crawl away as far as I can make it before I'm dragged back by an ankle.

Just as I'm turned and flipped over, a different man wearing a suit straddles me, jabbing me with a needle in my right arm. I feel pain as he injects me with mystery liquid and my body goes limp.

I'm in a place between waking and sleep, some sort of twilight zone, as I'm thrown into the backseat of a car. I whimper in fear as my body jolts and bounces off the seat, causing me to become nauseous again. Everything about this screams wrong, wrong, *wrong*. Why would they do this to me? And what exactly are they doing? I don't know where I'm going, but it doesn't seem like I'm having better luck than being trapped in a basement. The sound of the door slamming shut startles me out of my thoughts, but my limbs aren't responding so there's no outward reaction. *What did they give me?!*

Surely, they're going to kill me.

At least, I hope so.

The gentle rumble of the engine keeps me distracted, as well as my thoughts spiraling out of control over what my life will be like in the next second, minute, hour. But the ride is short, at least it seems that way in my mind, and the car stops abruptly. By the time a stranger opens my door, I can feel my legs again. I can *move* again.

Everyone is wearing suits. The driver, the man who opens my door, and the man in the passenger seat. They look important somehow, I just don't know why they would want me. An orphan who got taken in by an adoptive family just to be shoved in a basement for being disobedient. For not wanting to comply with their expectations of me. The truth is, my mother was never religious, and of course she didn't raise me to be. And how would she even make it to church? Most days she was too doped up on pills to even get out of bed. Sometimes the hunger in my belly felt like it was eating me alive. So yeah, no time for religion. Only time for survival. When I made it to my adoptive parents, I was rebelling against everything they said to do. Mostly because I didn't believe in it; I didn't want to believe in it either.

"Consequently, he who rebels against the authority is rebelling against what God has instituted, and those who do so will bring judgment on themselves."

Or so I've been told half my life.

It's been five days since I made it to this house after spending months in foster care. It's a surprise I was even adopted due to my age. I'm eleven now. But I've been told they're good people, God's people. I don't know what that means, I've never really learned about it. But they want me, and now, as I sit in this house, I think about how much it would please them to change my ways, but that only makes me nauseous.

"It's time for Sunday School," my foster mother says, her blonde hair and blue eyes looking like mine, and if you didn't know I was adopted, you'd think I was her biological daughter. Her blood. It's almost comforting, but it makes me more nervous than anything that she'd try to treat me like the rest of them. Have the same expectations of me that I will never be able to abide by. I won't ever be what they want me to be, I can't even be what I want me to be. "Let's go."

"No," I say defiantly. I raise my chin and square my shoulders. "My mom never made me do that."

"Listen here, brat." She grabs my cheeks forcefully, causing me to bite the inside of them, crushing my jaw. "You will do as we say or there will be consequences."

"No," I repeat.

My foster mother lets go of me and takes a step back, but just when I think she's going to walk away, she punches me in the face. Blood pours down my chin, from a split lip I'm sure, and I whimper, clutching at my jaw which feels like it's on fire.

"You," she says through her perfectly white gritted teeth, "will obey. For disobeying me is an insult to the Lord."

Where is God now? They just gave me over to these people, no questions asked? Aren't they supposed to be nice and pure and all things good?

The tall, suited man at the door—at least six feet tall, with rugged features and black eyes—grabs me by the arm and all but drags me out of the vehicle, causing me to stumble and trip on my own feet. I guess that means I'm not as mobile as I thought. He half carries, half drags me toward a massive airplane, and I try to plant my feet in a futile attempt at a refusal to move.

He doesn't even notice it.

My eyes widen as we ascend the steps that lead to the top, and because my legs feel like putty if it weren't for his tight grip on me, I'd be face-planting. Fear crawls down my spine like a thousand little spiders, biting and tickling, and I realize one thing: I've never been on a plane. Where the hell are they taking me?

It doesn't matter because as I walk in, I notice a bunch of other girls sitting down next to each other. They're all different races, and none of them look like me. Their clothes are tattered and dirty, and so are their faces. They look like they've been kidnapped, taken somehow. Like they've seen better days. And when a brunette with green eyes looks at me, all I see is sadness in her eyes. My heart hurts for her, constricting in my chest with a vice grip, and I swallow hard. I think this is what will become of me. No—I'm sure of it. And that knowledge doesn't make me feel any better. Right now, ignorance would be bliss.

There are four rows of seats, and three girls per row. Me? I guess I'm sitting alone because he drops me off in the row behind all of them. No one turns their head to look at me either after the brunette looks away, and I guess everyone is going to fend for themselves. They don't even make eye contact with each other.

The lightly humming cabin begins to purr, then whine. The plane starts to move, and I look around at the spacious and luxurious interior. It's impressive—everything is. Down to the brown leather seats at the very front, facing us. After a while the plane begins to move faster, as if it's driving, and it shakes violently the further we go. I wish I had someone with me, that I could hold a hand, as it stands this may be the scariest thing I've experienced. Maybe I don't like planes.

My stomach dips and I groan as we ascend. My ears begin to ring, then they start to pop. It's freaking miserable. The window seat at least gives me the ability to look down and see how far off the ground we are, which —bad idea.

Oh, God.

My stomach turns violently and I breathe in deeply, trying to not think of how far up in the air we are and how we could fall down to our deaths. Maybe that's how I'll die. Maybe I really am dying today.

Shaking my head and trying not to think of it, I crane my neck to try to get a better view of the front, where the suited men who brought me here walked to, but then they come right back and sit behind me, their guns showing on a holster at their hips. They seem to be some kind of security.

"Are you looking for someone?" the man behind me asks as I turn my body to the side and out of the seat, looking toward the front of the plane. "Is there something you'd like to see?"

I gasp when I see a man with his penis out, and a girl putting it in her mouth. His pants suit is down to his ankles and his head is thrown back with his mouth wide open. "N-n-o." He looks like power personified with his twinkling rings and suit, his dark hair neatly combed back. The man looks like he could be a politician, but surely I'm wrong.

"I guess if you're as pure as they say, then you've never seen a cock before."

Cock.

I almost scoff at the pureness jab, but I don't, too entranced and disgusted to reply. Looking away, I right myself in my seat and lean my head back, closing my eyes. This plane is fancy as hell with its leather chairs and spacious interior, and the men in the front all have women between their legs. Worse is the fact that everyone in front of me is tied up. Their hands and feet. It's no wonder they won't look at each other.

"Guess she got tired of watching," one of the men says, laughing at my expense. "Might as well take a break since she's probably next in line for it."

The man next to him laughs as well. "All of them are."

I keep my eyes closed and breathe in and out slowly, trying to even my breaths, and eventually, I'm back in a dazed state. I don't know if it's what they gave me or if I'm just exhausted, but I guess I fall back asleep. Then, when I wake again the plane is landing.

The wheels bounce off the ground repeatedly, jolting my body in the seat, and when we stop, I almost puke again. The suited men behind me start getting up and out of their seats, moving toward the front of the plane. There's hushed whispers coming from the girls in front of me. Most of them look like they're around my age or older, and multiple men begin to carry them out of the plane like sacks of potatoes.

What the fuck is going on? Who are these people? Where are we going? Are they taking us to the same place? And why am I the only one not tied up?

"Your turn." One of the suited men that was seated behind me announces, grabbing my arm. I don't resist though. I'm already where they want me—and I have no idea where that is so it's not like I can fight them.

They take me back down the steps of the airplane to a black limo where they stick me with all the other girls who are bound. For some reason they don't dare look at one another or me; they don't make one single sound. No one questions why I'm getting a little more special treatment than them, and I guess I should be grateful because I don't want to be hated for something I can't control.

The limousine takes off, and thankfully there are no men in here with us. It helps me breathe a little easier. I look out the window at the lush scenery. Wherever we are is really green and actually pretty. Not that I'll get to appreciate it much, I'm sure. For all I know everything looks green because I haven't seen trees in a decade, so nothing that impressive to anyone else I guess.

A while later we're pulling up to a house, no, a castle. A fucking castle. This place is a damn mansion with turrets—who has turrets on a house? It doesn't matter though because someone opens the door and

I'm yanked out by my arm. I guess it sucked that I've been sitting nearest the door. I'm assuming the special treatment is over now. I don't look back to see if the other girls are out or not, instead I continue to face forward and walk wherever I'm directed to—more like pulled to.

Anger floods my veins and I growl at him like a dog, a feral little creature. But he's unphased, and it makes me want to stab him right in the gut, where I can reach. I look around and see his gun, making the itch to grab it strong. Maybe if I'm quick, if he doesn't notice—

Do it.

No, don't.

I giggle.

God wouldn't like that.

You don't give a fuck about God.

Fuck, okay.

I right myself and keep being dragged toward the entrance of the home. The house is enormous, but I don't even have time to appreciate the pretty hardwood floors and traditional decor as I'm taken toward a hallway to an open door. Just as I'm about to be pushed through another door though, a familiar man comes out of the room.

White blond hair.

Striking blue eyes.

Straight nose.

Pouty lips.

Huge heart.

No.

I gasp and my hands begin to tremble, as does my

lower lip. His eyes widen once they take me in and his lips part.

"Drav—"

I stop myself, not understanding what kind of sick and twisted fucking game this is. Something tells me I'm about to find out in any case, and I'm about to hate my life.

CHAPTER TWO
DRAVEN

"F*irefly*."

I whisper so low I'm not sure she's heard me, though clearly she has by the way tears pool in her eyes.

"Oh, God." She sobs "I thought you were dead!"

My memories taunt me. The last one I have of us. Of her.

Firefly.

"God you feel so good, so perfect."

"It's just us forever, right?" She asks me, her doe eyes wide with tears as I thrust in and out of her. "Right?"

"Forever, baby."

Fuck, I failed her.

It wasn't forever back then, but I'm making up for it now. I need to take her and explain, I need to tell her what's happening, but I can't very well divulge the entire ritual. Only her part in it.

The Family is sacred and not to be betrayed.

Not for her, not for anyone.

"I'm not." I smile at her, but her lips just wobble more violently. I can see her hands shaking even from all these feet away, and a shiver runs down my spine. What if she doesn't love me anymore? What if she doesn't want me? What if another man got stuck in that fucking basement with her and I can't have her anymore? But see that's the thing, I'm not that nice, sweet, naive boy anymore. No, I take what I want now.

And I want *her*.

"You're more beautiful than when I left." I tell her honestly, noticing more curves than three years ago. Angel's waist is still small, with an hour-glass figure, and her tits still look about the same, perky and barely a handful. Perfect. Her beautiful blonde hair, the deepest blue of her eyes. They're the bluest eyes I've ever seen. Indigo. *Gorgeous.* "So perfect, baby." I repeat what I used to say to her. And she really is with her full lips, straight small nose, and heart-shaped face. A little cleft on her chin.

She gasps again. "How is this possible, Draven?" I look at her more closely. She's fucking pale and clearly vitamin deficient, but I'll be fixing that soon. I'm not surprised though, she's been in that basement for ten years. How the fuck did she not go crazy? Maybe she has. I don't fucking care. "How did you get me out of there? How long has it been?"

"Three years since I last saw you."

She cries again.

"It doesn't matter," I reply, and tears trail down her face, "Did you really think I'd let you go? That I wouldn't come back for you?" I walk closer to her until we're standing toe to toe. She's even more breathtaking up close with cute little freckles on her face. She'll look even more gorgeous underneath me, on top of me, however I can get her. "You're mine, Angel. I'll *never* let you go again."

"Sir," the enforcer says, someone I hadn't even noticed. He's just been standing on the sidelines listening to everything I've told her. I don't give a shit though, everyone should know not to fuck with her now that she's here. "I'm assuming you don't want me to take her to her quarters?"

"You're dismissed," I reply coldly, wanting her to myself already. This was the plan all along, to be with her, to never be without her again. She's it for me, always has been. Always will be. I promised her forever and I plan to deliver. In just a few days.

Angel stays rooted to the spot, completely unmoving. Shit, I don't even think she's breathing right now. "Come here, Angel," I tell her, calling her by her name, trying not to freak her out more than she already is. Surprisingly, she wraps her arms around me, squeezing my middle. Her head reaches just below my chin. She's always been tall. I'd say five-seven or eight. "Did you miss me?"

Like a dam has broken free, she begins to sob against me. My eyes prick with my own tears, and I rub her back as her body shakes. "So. Fucking. Much," she replies, making me chuckle.

"When did my little Firefly start cursing?" I ask her with amusement, my lips quirking up even through my tears. "The Angel I know doesn't cuss."

"A lot has changed since then, Drav."

My body heats at her nickname for me, coming back just like that. So effortlessly that it makes me hopeful. Maybe she hasn't moved on after all, not that I care if she has.

"Come with me." I take a step back and begin to tug her to the opposite side of the house. I take her up a set of stairs and to the right of the hallway, to my room. She doesn't say anything, just looks at the floor, not even looking at the pretty house. It's an impressive home, with blonde hardwood floors and modern decor. I feel lucky every day to have the opportunity to be here, and also have a lavish house of my own, considering the shit hole I came from.

"What is this place? Is this where I'm staying?" She asks with apprehension in her voice as I close the door behind us. She doesn't trust this. Or me. I need to change that considering the bomb I'm about to drop on her.

"This is my bedroom, Firefly." I drag her to my bed and sit her down. "And we can't stay together until...after."

"After what?"

Uh, how do I answer that? How do I tell her that I bought her from her parents and they gave her over like she was nothing? How do I tell her I belong to a secret society, a fucking cult, and the only way to protect her and have her be a part of my life is through marriage? Through the consecration of it?

This is proving to be more difficult than I expected.

"Angel, I have something to tell you." I need to

figure out a way not to give too much away. She immediately stiffens, her blue eyes narrowing on my own. "After your parents kicked me out onto the street, I was adopted by the family who owns this house."

She gasps for the millionth time. "That's incredible!"

I nod my head yes, because I feel very lucky. "They are very powerful people. I'm saying...they hold key positions in the U.S. government that I can't divulge yet."

Like Secretary of State.

Senators.

This cult controls the government, every aspect of it, it's monopolized. All decisions go through The Fellowship, they've made sure of it, and eventually they'll go through The Heathens too when the time comes. When we graduate from graduate school and we're given our own positions in the government. It's possible I may start out at the state government level before moving up to the federal government, but I'll get there eventually. I'm still young. I'll be a senior next year and move on to law school, then everything will fall into place. I will know exactly what I'll be doing with my life. At least for the next few years.

"And why is that?"

"Because they won't trust you until..." You belong to The Family. Until you have no choice. Until there's no way out because you've married into a fucking cult that you can't get out of. Not alive. We live and die by the rules. We inhale and exhale The Heathens. "...you're mine in every way." The Fellowship consists of thirteen founding families and The

Heathens are their children. My father is the leader of The Fellowship, the *Dux*, and consequently my adoptive brother Killian is the leader of The Heathens as first born. Together, we consist of The Family.

"How did I get here, Draven?" she asks carefully, and even her eyes are guarded. I think she's beginning to understand that something about this is important even if she doesn't know how yet. "Why am I here?"

How do I say this in a way that lets her down easy? I can't. There are no words that can make this better. "Your parents let me have you if I gave them something in return."

Angel shakes her head. "What? What did they accept in return?" The hurt on her face is enough to bring me to my knees in front of her. I kneel and take her hands in mine.

"Money."

Her breath whooshes out. "No way. They don't care about that. God wouldn't approve."

"Fuck God!" I snap. I've never believed in Him or the teachings they shoved down my throat. Where the fuck was He when we were stuck in that basement for years? "They did it, Angel. You're here, aren't you? Do you really believe they'd just let you go out of the good-ness of their hearts? No. Not after locking you up for that long. So fuck them."

"But why am I here? Why did you want me to come here with *you*?"

I reach up to touch her hair. "Because I could finally get you back. I'm in a good place, baby. I'm powerful too. I'll be getting a government position when I'm done with school."

"Are you rich?"

I smile. "I'm more than rich, baby." I try to think of words that won't freak her out too much. "With excellence comes wealth, and with wealth comes power." That's something my father has ingrained into my brain for years now.

She's stunned into silence with that, and her chest begins to heave a little.

"You're here to be my wife, baby." *Mine*. "Don't be scared, Firefly." I stroke her cheek and she shivers. "It was the only way out of your fucking prison." And your only way into a new one.

"Wife?" she squeaks, her voice smaller than I've ever heard before. Like she's scared. I guess she should be. The marriage ritual is nothing like Christian weddings. "I'm twenty-one years old, Draven! Shouldn't we take this a little bit slower? Give ourselves more time?"

"I've loved you forever, Angel. No age will keep me from making you mine."

"I'm already yours, Draven," she mumbles. "You don't need marriage to prove it."

"You're right. But we need marriage to be able to keep you here."

Angel frowns. "I don't understand."

"I can't explain, yet. I'm sorry." I plead with my eyes. "Please. Just let me take care of you."

I come to my feet and pull her off the bed, the white boring sheets creasing a bit from her moving on them. Everything is white in here, stale. Although it's my bedroom, I don't live here anymore. I have my own house. So I really could care less about how it looks.

Every bedroom in this house is built the same way for maximum privacy. In fact, it's like a hotel suite where there's a door that leads to a private living room and a dining area.

"This place is like a castle," she says in awe and I chuckle.

I see how she'd think that, and once upon a time, I did too. I was so amazed by this place it clouded my judgment a lot. Not that I've had a choice in a lot of things, no, they've made the decisions for me and I've followed along because without them I'd be nothing. It's loyalty to death.

"It is," I reply with a smile. "But all I care about is you. Being with you is my priority. If I lose everything today—this castle—nothing would matter except for you, baby."

Her eyes water, tears spilling down her cheeks. "I want us back."

"You have us back, Firefly." Her smile at that lights up my world. "Now let's go in the shower and get you out of these clothes. We need to wash that fucking basement off your pretty skin."

I direct her to the bathroom, the white tiles cold under my feet, and she closes the door behind us. "This is crazy, Drav. I've never seen anything like it before."

"It is crazy. But you know what's crazier?" I ask her and she looks at me, "You being here with me."

I let go of her hand and go in the shower, turning all shower heads to almost hot water. I don't know her shampoo anymore, not that she's had many choices of it, but I still remember her soap. Peach Bellini. I wonder if she'll still smell like herself once she's showered with mine or if it will completely disappear. I've been waiting for her to get here so I can go buy all her essentials.

"Come on, Angel," I call out to her as I step out of the shower. "Let me help you shower." She glances between me and the shower, noticing the glass enclosure, and she looks shy all of a sudden.

"Um." She clears her throat. "Isn't it *weird* to do that? We haven't seen each other in so long."

"Weird? No." I shake my head. "I've waited a long time for this. *Please*," I beg her.

Angel nods, beginning to slip off her shoes, then takes her shirt and pants off until she stands in the raggedy underwear they've been making her wear. Never again will she lack for anything. Over my dead fucking body.

She looks at the ground for a moment, standing without making eye contact with me. I hate it. Where is my girl? Where did she go? Why did her light go off? She's my Firefly. She's happiness personified.

I get closer to her and clasp my hands around her shoulders, "May I?" I ask her softly, and she nods.

I unclasp the back of her bra, removing it from her body and letting it drop to the ground. Ready to worship all of her, I get on my knees and hook my thumbs into her panties, slowly lowering them. I don't know what I was expecting, but having her bare before my eyes wasn't it. Even though she's been captive she's had great hygiene, and I guess some habits just can't be broken.

Dropping her underwear all the way to her ankles, she then steps out of them. I catch her scent deep in my nostrils, and I groan. She smells like... her. Like sweetness and peaches and her.

"Fuck." I press my nose against her and inhale deeply, wrapping my arms around her legs and squeezing her ass softly. "I've missed you so much."

Her fingers grip my hair, tightening around it until my eyes water, but I don't care. As long as she's the one causing my pain I'd be okay with going through it.

"Get up," she tells me, her voice hoarse. "I want to see you, too."

There's my girl. As possessive as I am, she's always been the one in charge. In charge of my heart. I oblige, getting up from the tiled floor and stripping my clothes off. I don't wait for her though. Instead, I get in the shower and dip my head under the hot water. It's steaming in here, the cloud of fog rising from the bottom, and I barely see her when she steps in, until she's right in front of me in all her glorious beauty.

She looks at me unabashedly, her eyes trailing from my toes up and lingering on my cock. I smile at that, and her eyes snap up to mine. Her cheeks burn, and the pretty bubblegum blush makes me want to put her in my pocket and keep her there forever.

"You look," I can hear her just barely over the spray of water from three different shower heads, but she raises her voice at the last part, "like a man."

I smirk, then close the distance between us, grabbing her jaw with my fingertips and tilting her head up to mine. Her indigo eyes dilate, the black blowing up and swallowing the blue, and her mouth parts for me. I take her lips with mine, gently probing until she molds herself against me. Taking her hand, I direct it to my cock and wrap her fist around it, moving it up and down slowly. She moans at that, and I take advantage of it by slipping my tongue into her mouth. She tastes so fucking good.

"I *am* a man now, baby," I tell her when I pull away, and she doesn't let go of me. "I'm yours."

"Mine?"

I pull her hand off me and sink to my knees, looking up at her. "Have you been good for me? All these years?" I bring her leg over my shoulder, exposing her to me. Her pink pussy is glistening with need, and satisfaction fills me. I look up at her eyes, which are sparkling with that old light between us. Her eyes glisten and she bites her bottom lip.

"Always."

"Do you want this?" I ask her, taking a tentative lick. She jumps a little and I pull away. "Do you want me?"

"Yes, please. I've missed you. Take what you want."

"*Ask me,*" I demand.

"For what?" There's a frown on her face.

"Ask me to take you."

"*Please*, Drav." She all but begs. "*Take* me. Make me feel good. Make me forget about my life."

I descend on her like a starved man. And starved I really fucking am as I take her clit between my lips and suck on it lightly. I alternate between sucks and licks, not wanting to overwhelm her since it's been a long time since she's done this.

She props herself against the wall, her head resting against it with her leg slung over my shoulder and closes her eyes. With one hand I hold onto her leg, and with the other I take my cock in my hand and begin to pump it.

Angel's moans are loud, echoing off the bathroom walls, and I jerk off harder, faster, to the pace of how I'm licking her. They sound even better than when she was eighteen, throatier, huskier. Now I can't control my damn self after I see how crazy I'm making her. Her leg tightens around me and her hands come to my hair, ripping at the strands as she begins to ride my face.

Fucking hell.

My spine begins to tingle, my balls drawing up, and just as her legs begin to shake I come all over the shower floor. She screams, pulling my hair, and I moan as the last drop of my cum hits the ground.

"Oh." She sighs as I extricate her from me. "*Draven*."

"I know, baby."

I turn off the shower heads and grab the towel from the nearest hook. White and fluffy and large just for her, then I dry her thoroughly. I carry her to my bed and give her my shirt, all the while dripping water across my suite. But I don't give a shit, she will always come first. Or as first as she can be.

Angel gets dressed in my black t-shirt—which swallows her whole as it comes down to mid-thigh—and then curls up in my bed like she's exhausted. She probably is considering the amount of hours it took to get her here to Silent Grove, Virginia. The little town she lived in, Salem, Alabama is in the middle of nowhere. But now she's here and I'm never letting her go.

She falls asleep quickly, her deep breaths filling the space between us, yet making me feel hollow all over again. I get dressed and climb in next to her, but I don't let sleep claim me. Instead, I watch her. Her breaths echo in my ears, the way her little nostrils flare as she takes them in and out. Angel's closed eyes flutter behind her lids, and I hope she's dreaming of us. I don't look at the time or know how long I've been staring at her; all I know is that I'm still in awe of her. All these years later, and nothing has changed. At least not for me.

An alarm rings on my phone and I look at it, unable to remember why I set it, but even still I sit up in bed, and she does too. "What is that?"

"An alarm, Firefly."

"Oh," she mumbles with furrowed brows. "I'm hungry," she says as her stomach growls and her face heats.

"Let's find you something to eat, okay?"

"Okay."

We get out of bed and open the door, stepping out of the bedroom and closing it behind us. For some reason my adoptive brother and soulmate's door is open —which he doesn't usually leave that way—and just as we're about to pass it he steps out of the room.

Completely naked.

And with a hard dick.

What. The. Fuck.

He makes no move to cover himself, instead he has a smile playing on his lips and a twinkle in his eye that makes me want to fucking destroy him.

And I swear on my life I will if he fucks with me and her.

CHAPTER THREE

KILLIAN

"We have a screamer among us," I say to Draven, while leering at her. Her face heats, and she glares at me like she wants to stab me, blue eyes flashing. Her perfect lips purse after a moment of me watching her, and I look down her body to appreciate her figure. I don't even try to hide it as my eyes linger on her perky little tits, then her thin waist and slightly curvy body. A goddess.

"Shut the fuck up." He growls and my smile turns into a grin. "Let's go, Angel."

"Angel, huh?" I ask her, and her eyes narrow on me but she doesn't say anything still. I kind of like her bratty nature; she'd look good on her knees for me. She doesn't look like an angel though, she looks like a beautiful demon waiting to be summoned. A fucking brat underneath all her layers. "I'm Kill. Nice to meet you."

At that she nods, her eyes softening slightly. Her eyes are so deeply blue I begin to get lost in them, then shake myself out of it. "Nice to meet you too."

"If you can go put on some clothes, please." Draven

rolls his eyes in irritation and I chuckle, going back to my room. He knows damn well I'm naked most of the time, or at least half-naked. Before I close the door he says, "I need you to help me keep her company for an hour while I run an errand."

Perfect.

"So you want me to be your babysitter? I may be your soulmate, but even they don't pay me enough for that."

"Watch your mouth, Killian," he snaps. "There are some things I haven't explained."

"Oh?" I raise an eyebrow at him. "Whatever, I'll keep her." I wink, yet I find myself meaning it. Maybe I want what he could have but doesn't yet. Maybe I really *will* keep her.

"Just keep your mouth shut." He huffs and I close my door to get dressed.

I'll be honest, I don't intend to keep my mouth shut. Instead, I want to run it. I want to make her trust me, though I don't think it'll happen in such a short period of time.

According to Draven, he hasn't told her much, which I think is so irresponsible. If she were mine I'd tell her much more, if only to keep her safe. I wouldn't tell her everything, but enough to appease her and give her an idea of what the hell she's getting into. Is he even giving her a choice? I wouldn't give her one, not really. I'd just let her know she's going to be part of something much more powerful—bigger—than she can imagine.

I think I'm not going to keep my mouth shut at all.

Putting on a pair of gray sweats that hang low on my

hips, I throw the door open for Angel. Draven scowls when her eyes linger on me and her face heats.

"Can't you wear a shirt?" he asks, gesturing with his hand at my naked torso.

"No. It's this or nothing."

I kind of want to taunt her, see if I affect her even a little bit. I don't know why though, maybe I'm just bored. This could be fun, especially because it's really pushing Draven's buttons. I do love pushing his buttons, I love everything about it.

"Whatever," he mutters. "Just watch her and don't let anyone talk to her until I get home."

That I do have to agree with. Our father is a scary motherfucker, and she doesn't need to be intimidated yet. She will be when she's part of the marriage ritual. As *Dux*, the leader, he will be in charge of conducting the marriage ceremony, and well the other part of it. Until she's married, she technically doesn't have the right to know shit. But I'm going to divulge a few secrets.

Vivimus per praecepta, morimur per praecepta.

We live by the rules, we die by the rules.

I won't break any, I'll just *bend* them.

Like I want to do to her, too.

I step out of the way and she enters my bedroom cautiously, as if I might bite her and take a chunk out. She's not wrong, I could. I *want* to. Either way, her chin is raised high and there's strength in her gait, not cowering at all.

Angel walks in just as Draven walks away without looking back. I could easily take her to the living room just beyond my room, but I don't want to. For some sick, twisted reason I want her in my bed.

I gesture to the bed and say, "Get comfortable, baby girl."

Her eyes snap up to mine again, and her face burns anew. She seems uncomfortable and I fucking love it. I want her on edge around me, always unsure of my next move. Whether I'll be nice or a fucking asshole. Whether I'll make her feel good or used and abused.

"On the bed?" She looks at the black silk sheets for a moment, then around at the dark gray walls. Unlike my brother, I actually care about how this room looks, no matter if I have my own house or not. If I'm going to spend any amount of time here, I'm going to mark it with *me*.

"Do you see any other furniture?"

She breathes in deeply. "Is there nowhere else to go?"

I chuckle at her boldness already, the little attitude she has with me because I've annoyed her. "Nowhere I want to take you."

"Fine." She all but stomps toward the bed and crawls across it, settling in on the side where I sleep. There's already pillows propped up and she sits up against the headboard, arranging them to where she's comfortable. I look at her for a bit, admiring her, and she turns her head to glance at me with narrowed eyes. "Are you going to stare at me all day?"

"Maybe." I wink, getting on the bed beside her. We look at each other, and I'll give it to her, she's braver than I thought. She doesn't hesitate at all as she maintains eye contact and lifts her chin. She's feisty, this one. "You're very pretty."

Her face heats again. I think this girl never stops blushing, or maybe she's pissed off. "How about we start over? Because I don't think Draven would appreciate you calling me pretty."

"I don't think you know what he appreciates."

She raises an eyebrow. "Oh, I think I know more than you think."

Oh.

Interesting. Here I thought she was a virgin just like the other girls they brought with her. It makes her a little more out of reach, yet so much more enticing. I've always liked a challenge, a game.

"I'm Killian." I grin, winking at her as I reintroduce myself.

"Angel."

"No, you're not. You're the prettiest demon I've ever seen in my life." It's true. She's unholy, no part of her is angelic. Her name must be a contradiction, and I bet once I peel off a few layers she'll show me I'm right. She'll unleash whatever hell she harbors inside.

Angel scoffs, "A demon?"

"A little one." She smiles at that, the first real one she gives me, and it feels like a gift. I don't overthink it though. Instead, I get up from the bed. "Are you hungry?"

"Starving." Her lips set into a thin line, almost like she's embarrassed to admit it. Why would she feel that way though? Where did she come from anyway? It's weird the way they brought her here, with all the other sacrifices. Yet she's not with them at all.

"I'll make you something real quick."

I don't know much about cooking, but I have a few things I can whip up in the kitchen, one of them being grilled cheese. You can't really fuck that up anyway, I don't think. So I pass her the remote and go to the kitchenette just beyond the bedroom, getting a flat pan and everything set up. There's a small pantry with some canned soups I keep for those midnight munchies when I smoke pot, at least for when I'm trying to be healthy. I pour tomato soup into a bowl and heat it up in the microwave, then put the bread and cheese on the pan.

Something I can't explain makes me want to get to know this girl, and she might just be vulnerable enough right now to give me some scraps of information. In return, I'll give her some scraps of mine. I won't give her everything though. How do I explain that she'll be part of a marriage ritual where everyone will witness the consummation of her union? That she will have to watch some depraved shit happen? How do I tell her that the girls she came with are all part of a virgin sacrifice for our fucked up cult?

Not that it matters.

Nothing will change her fate now, except maybe me. As for the cult? Some may call it an academic secret society, but we all know the truth, at least the ones that are in it. There are many layers to it, a clear-cut hierarchy. Three levels to this. The Fellowship, which consists of the heads of thirteen families, the *Dux* as the head of

The Fellowship. They are in charge of us and the lower sect.

At my level, we have The Heathens, which consists of six of us. All six of us are divided into pairs, soulmates, and one of us leads as well. I'm the leader of The Heathens since my father is *Dux*, and Draven is my soulmate. The Fellowship and The Heathens are *The Family*, as every Heathen is the son of a Fellow. At the lower sect, we have The Vipers, which are the underdogs. They do the dirty work that we keep our hands clean of. They take care of the weapons and drug trade, human trafficking, organ trafficking and the black market.

You see, our society is special. The Fellowship are all politicians, and that's exactly what they expect of us as well. Merit is rewarded, and there are high expectations for us. In return, when the time comes, we will have positions of power and more money than we could dream of. More opportunities than we could even imagine.

All we have to do is follow directions.

Obey without question.

Blindly trust.

Then all of our dreams will come true. It's not that hard to turn a blind eye, every organization is corrupt. Ours is no different.

I finish up in the kitchen and return to the bedroom, handing Angel her food and sitting next to her. I have every intention of extracting information, but I can't help but watch as her eyes widen at the food and feel a pang of something unfamiliar in my chest.

Pity. Why is she looking at grilled cheese that way? It feels...sad. Like I'm intruding on a very intimate moment between her and a fucking sandwich.

"Maybe you won't like this." I look into her deep blue eyes as I say to her, "But you could dip it in the tomato soup."

Angel makes a very confused face but dips her grilled cheese, then takes a very tentative bite. She moans softly and I shift uncomfortably on the bed, trying to adjust myself without being vulgar.

I really shouldn't be lusting over my baby brother's soon-to-be wife, but I've never been a good person. I've never liked the things I should. There's something seriously wrong with me. I'm wired all fucking wrong.

Fuck.

She gets some tomato soup all over one finger, and I curse myself for forgetting to bring a napkin with me. It doesn't matter though because I take her hand and put her finger in my mouth, sucking it softly. She pulls her slender hand away and gasps, her mouth parted and her eyes wide. Damn...I don't know what's gotten into me.

"Stop." She breathes. "You can't do that."

"Why not? I was just helping you out, baby girl."

"You *know* why not."

But I see the way her eyes betray her, lingering on my body. Especially on my torso, at my snake tattoos, the brand on the left side of my chest—the skull with the snake coming out of the eyes and mouth—that signifies my place in this cult.

We all have it. The Heathen tattoo right below my collarbones, the Eye of Providence right below it—an eye within a triangle with rays of sunlight. But her eyes trail lower, betraying her, and they linger on my abs, on the colorful devil tattoo right below at my sweatpants waistline that leads right to my cock. Then her eyes trail even lower. She swallows thickly, like she's salivating at the sight. I harden immediately and her eyes widen.

"Careful, little demon." I tsk. "I might get the wrong idea if you keep looking at me that way."

She deflects. "What is that on your chest?" I look down, knowing exactly what she's talking about but refusing to acknowledge it until she asks me directly. "The skull with the snake coming out of it?"

"A brand."

"As in, someone burned you?" I nod. "Like cattle?"

"Exactly." I grin, thinking of how right she is. Though we're more like sheep being herded wherever The Fellowship says.

"Why?" She gulps. "Draven has it too."

I hesitate, because how do I explain without giving it all away? "We're part of something...bigger than ourselves."

"He said as much, but just what the hell are you part of?"

"You could call it...a society." *A cult.* "And once you're married, you will also be part of it by association. We don't exactly initiate women, since it's an all-male society. But because of marriage, you'll have certain knowledge of the ins and outs. Not everything, but enough to understand a lot of what happens."

She nods as if she understands, but her confusion shows in her eyes.

"Draven and I are the sons of Silas Hansen. He is the Attorney General of the Department of Justice."

"Like...The Cabinet?"

Smart girl. "Did you pay close attention to your government class?"

"Yes. I love anything related to the government."

"Well, this society is part of that." She may not love it for much longer. "They put us in positions of power, and in return we give back."

"What do they give you?"

"Anything we want." I chuckle at her curiosity. "Call it a scholarship. We get our tuition paid for in college —*in full*—and we also get accepted to whatever grad school we want."

"And do you *want* to go to grad school?"

"I'm already in graduate school right now. We all have to do it, we have no choice. One day I will be mayor of this city. Then Governor of Virginia." I smile at her as she sets her empty bowl down on the bed, too engrossed in our conversation. "I'm studying law while Draven studies pre-law at Mystic University. That's where we go, right here in Silent Grove, outside of the District. And he will be part of the Judicial branch of Virginia when everything is said and done, paving the way for us. Eventually, we will move up to the federal government. Think of us as the mafia, but fancier."

She now nods in understanding, and this time I do believe she has understood at least a portion of it. "What is the District?"

"You have a lot of questions, don't you?" I grin but humor her. "It's a neighborhood where the elite of

Silent Grove reside. All the politicians and their kids live here. We're thirty minutes outside of D.C."

"Like the capital?"

I grin. "Yes, little demon."

"Stop calling me that." Angel snaps and it makes me laugh, but she seems unaffected now. Yeah, she's greedy for information. "And where do you live when you're going to school? Here?"

"My house."

"What about when Draven and I are married? Can I go to school there?"

"I don't know about any of that." But instead, I want to say: If you were my wife, I'd keep you hidden so no one can look at how pretty you are. I'd want you all to myself. "School is almost out for fall break for just a few days, but we have more important matters to attend to...like your marriage ceremony."

Her eyes suddenly have a fearful look, and I tilt my head to the side. Does she not want to marry him? They seemed really cozy earlier. Her screams are still echoing in my head, and my cock threatens to go rock-hard again just imagining them again. What would she look like naked? Would her creamy skin bruise easily if I inflicted pain? *Snap out of it*.

"What about the marriage ceremony?"

"You need to be ready for it," I tell her. "You can't show weakness. They'll eat you alive if you do. That's all I will divulge for now, I'm sure Draven will fill you in on more details."

"Fine, then answer me this." She turns her body toward mine, then grabs my face and digs her nails into my cheeks. "Who were those girls and why were they tied up?"

"That's the one thing I can't tell you," I reply, and her nails dig in deeper. Well, there's much more I cannot say, but I can't tell her that. "But why did you come along with them? Shouldn't you know?"

"Draven bought me."

"*Bought* you?" I raise a brow. "Who the fuck from?"

She's silent for a beat, and I pry her hand from my face. I mirror her in return, using the same punishing hold on her. Except with my strength she whimpers and closes her eyes.

"My adoptive parents."

"Why did he buy you from them? Why would he have to? You seem to be grossly in love with each other." I don't believe in love, but the way he looks at her is disgusting—like he can't stand to be without her. I can tell she's so much more than what he's telling me. I'd even go as far as saying the love of his life, which only pisses me off.

I let go of her face.

"Because they had me locked up in a basement for a decade!" she snaps, clearly agitated. Her teeth are grinding, her jaw clenched, her hands balled into fists. "Is that what you wanted to know? That he saved me? That I'm grateful and that's why I'm agreeing? That I don't have a choice because that's the only reason he got me out?"

I look down at her heaving chest, stunned into silence. "A basement?" Is all I can get out.

"That's where I met him, you know?" No, I don't

fucking know shit. Draven didn't fill me in on this part of his life. "He was locked in there with me." There are parts of his life he seems to keep under wraps, I've always known that—that he had a hard life before my father met him and saw his potential, therefore making him one of his sons. But he's never trusted me the way I want him to—*need* him to. I've always needed him.

"It sounds like you feel you owe him a debt. For getting you out, rescuing you." I pin her to the bed and she closes her eyes, breathing heavily. Her palms meet my chest and she digs her fingernails into it.

I look down to find a trail of blood coming from below her fingernails, and I grin. It begins to wander all the way down to the waistline of my sweatpants, meeting the red devil tattoo. Perfect. I fucking love her violence. "If you want to marry someone else then say that now." Her eyes snap open, momentarily shocked, but her face turns determined once more, her nails digging in deeper right below my brand on the one side, a snake tattoo on the other.

"I don't!" she all but growls at me. "I. Don't. Want."

"Suit yourself," I grind out, getting on top of her and pinning my hips against hers, bringing my face closer until our lips are brushing. "Just let me know if you change your mind. Draven may love you, but you can be a true queen, ruling with me. "

If she knew anything about the ritual she wouldn't stay here, she'd run as far away as possible even if it meant dying. Not that it would matter much because Draven would likely find her. Or me.

And if I found her, I'd keep her.

I wrap my hand around her throat and she swallows against it. She's so fucking pretty, it's unfair, and I've never even been partial to blondes. We look at each other for a long moment and she tries to pry my fingers off with hers, but I just tighten my hold. I can't help myself, I fucking crash my lips against hers. She whimpers at first as I take her, her lips firm, but then she softens for me and my lips mold against hers.

When she relaxes, I loosen my hold on her neck, cupping her cheeks with both hands instead as I deepen the kiss, rocking my hips into hers. I suck her bottom lip into my mouth then slip my tongue inside, coaxing a moan from deep in her throat.

That little noise almost undoes me until I hear the doorknob turning and I pry myself from her, throwing my body to the other side of the bed. Her chest is heaving and her eyes are narrowed at me, and just as my brother walks in through the door he stops in his tracks. I look back at him with a smile and he raises his brows.

"Let's go, Angel."

At his command, Angel begins to get up from the bed. I get closer to her and whisper in her ear. "Tell your little love what just happened, baby girl. Or I'm going to keep you all to myself."

And as she walks out, I decide I have to have her.

I just need to figure out how.

CHAPTER FOUR

ANGEL

I've already been here for two days, and I'm more confused than I've ever been in my entire twenty-one years on this earth. I don't know what I'm getting myself into, but if there's this much secrecy, it can't be good. Draven hasn't told me how we're getting married, just that it's tomorrow and it won't be a *traditional* wedding.

Whatever the hell that means.

What's even more confusing is how Killian treated me two days ago. He made me food, he explained things to me that Draven had kept from me. He fucking kissed me. Then he told me to tell Draven what happened.

Fuck. *No*.

He must be out of his mind if he thinks I'll sabotage what I have with Draven. Over what? A kiss he forced on me? No matter how much I melted against him and wished for more, it was wrong. I shouldn't be thinking about him, I should be focused on the man who rescued me. My everything.

And it won't be happening again.

No, the only one I'll be fucking is Draven, who is right here in this bed with me, looking straight into my eyes. His striking ones dilate and constrict once more as he looks at me, and he licks his lips.

I follow a line down his torso, his brand on the left side of his chest. A Heathen tattoo below his collarbones right where Killian's is. Black butterflies flying up his torso—and I immediately know why they're there.

We used to talk about butterflies coming out of cocoons. His new *beginning*. Random tattoos litter his torso, snakes on his hips leaning down, down, down to his cock. Killian has tattoos there, too. I lick my lips, snapping my eyes back to his.

"There's something you're not telling me," I say softly, and he tenses.

"There's *too much* I'm not telling you, Angel." He kisses me softly then pulls back. "But you have to accept that until you're my wife, my lips are sealed."

"Why?"

"Because there are rules for everything, and this is what they call for."

"You and your fucking rules," I scoff. "What will I wear for this wedding? Can you even tell me what I'll be doing?"

Draven gulps, running a hand through his white blond hair. "Nothing," he whispers.

Oh, hell no. "You mean to tell me that I will be naked in front of people I don't even know?" There's no way I can do this. "And they what? Get off on it?"

"It's the rules—"

"*Fuck* your rules, Draven!" I growl at him. "I will not go naked. How many people?"

"Thirty." He looks down. "Maybe more."

In a moment of madness, I flip him onto his back, climb on top and straddle his hips, rubbing my pussy against his hardening dick. "Do you really want to show me off, Drav?" I ask him in a breathy voice that makes him push up against me, trying to seek some friction. "You want everyone to see me naked?"

He grabs my face, squeezing my cheeks, hurting me. It brings little butterflies all the way to my pussy. "Of course not, Firefly. But I. Don't. Have. A. Choice."

"And why is that?"

"Because these people make all the decisions for me."

I stay silent and debate what he's saying. Is this what our whole life will be like? Following instructions? Not having any autonomy? I might as well be trapped in that basement again, the little girl with no way out.

"I know what you're thinking, Angel." Draven forces me to make eye contact with him. "I'll give you everything you could ever dream of, and even what won't ever cross your mind. Please trust me."

"I do," I reply carefully. "But I can't be trapped again."

"You won't be," he assures me. "I will give you the world if you let me, I'd give you *everything*." He growls, his free hand gripping my waist tightly, pinching my skin, digging his fingernails into it. I moan, my eyes going wide at his possessive grip.

"I feel the darkness closing in, Draven. I feel it again

and I don't like it. This whole situation where I'm going into this marriage blindly and into a fucking secret society—"

He frowns, his eyebrows drawing in, his mouth turning down. His voice is cold, summoning a chill down my spine. "So Killian has been filling your ears with bullshit now?"

"Is it bullshit, Draven?" I gasp as he rolls my hips over his, letting go of my face and his fingers digging into them. He's gentle, and I want more. He is *distracting* me from this conversation, and I'm letting him. Damn it all to fucking hell. Damn him for making me want him. "Or do you want to keep me in the dark like I've been my entire life?"

"The darkness is necessary for now, Angel."

I groan from annoyance and pleasure intertwined, and my hand meets his cheek gently. "Will you protect me?" What is going on? What will tomorrow look like for me? Is it going to change my life? Will I be branded too?

"Always." Draven reaches for my throat with one hand and pulls me down until our noses are touching. "You're my hope in the darkness, Firefly." That makes me feel slightly better. I have him. I have *him*.

Draven reaches between us to lower his pants, and I get off him momentarily. His big, hard, cock springs free, bobbing up to meet his abdomen. He's beautiful, a masterpiece. His snake tattoos extend all the way from his abs, to his hips, and down to his pelvis, right above his cock, a light dusting of hair right over them. I was too busy getting fucked by his tongue before to notice him. Really see him. I lift my shirt over my head and sit back on his thighs, baring myself to him as well. Grabbing my small breasts and squeezing them.

"God, you've never been more perfect than you are right now." He licks his lips. "Show me how shameless you are, baby. Let me see that tight little body." Softly, he trails his fingers down my waist until they reach my underwear, and he tears them down the middle and yanks them off. "Love me, Angel." He whispers, "Let *me* love you."

I hover over him until his cock is between us, hard and ready. It's been years since we've had sex, but I want to see the look of bliss on his face as *I'm* the one who fucks *him*. Exactly as it used to be. I love being the one he breaks over. "There will be no loving tonight." I lick my lips as I shift up and begin to move my hips back and forth, rubbing myself all over him. "I'm fucking you."

Draven's eyes flare with uncontained lust, and it makes my stomach flip. I feel a rush of warmth all the way to my pussy, and I rub a little faster. My center is slick with need, ready for him, yet he makes no move to rush me as he throws his head back, eyes closed and mouth open. He's panting underneath me, another sign of how much I affect him, and I go even faster. "Yes, baby, *fuck* me." His hands come to my ass, his finger brushing against my puckered hole, and he looks down between us. "I want to see that tight little pussy gripping me for all I'm worth."

I lift up off him and catch my breath for a second, trying to cool down the heat in my blood, the one that tells me to straddle him again and take what I want. Instead, I let him edge the head of his cock against my entrance. No matter how wet I am, it feels impossible as he slips in an inch.

Draven hisses, "Fuck, Firefly. I think I'll come before I'm all the way in if you don't relax."

"I *am* relaxed." I lie, feeling the burn as he stretches me. God, it's been so long.

"Liar." He chuckles, "But if it makes it easier, I'll make this quick for us."

"Okay." I say as I nod my head, only because this feels like torture. I want him inside me, but it feels like my body is rebelling, not wanting to let him in at all.

He grabs hold of my hips and begins to bounce me on his cock softly, and I feel myself give way for him. My muscles don't clamp around him anymore, in fact, they relax and take him in. When he's almost all the way, he slams me down until my clit hits his pelvis.

I moan, "*Drav*—"

"Does it feel good, baby?" He growls, his eyes closing tightly like he's fighting something inside himself. "Do you like how my cock is stretching you? You're so fucking tight. You're gripping me." He exhales. "So. Fucking. Good."

"Yessss," I breathe as he begins to pump me up and down on his cock. "Put your hands above your head." I smile sweetly at him, and he opens his eyes. "*Now*."

His hands come up above his head and he grabs the pillow with white knuckles. I grip his chest with my hands, closing my fingers around his skin until he hisses again. Up and down was good, but I don't think I can come that way. Instead, I go in circles until my clit brushes against his pelvis with every stroke, the little friction of his short hair making my legs tighten around his hips as I keep up the pace.

"So fucking good, Firefly," Draven praises. "Just like that baby. I *love* that—"

"Oh, God, Draven." I moan as I move faster. "*Drav.*"

My clit continues to rub against him, faster and faster. Harder. Animalistic sounds come out of me as I keep up the pace, and I bend down so he can suck on my tits. He gets the hint and opens wide, and lightning strikes down my back when he sucks me into his mouth. My pussy tightens, his cock stroking all the right places. I'm shameless just like he asked me to be, demanded. And I give him all my sounds, gift them to him.

He lets go of my tit and bites his lip on a groan, drawing blood. "You're almost there, baby. Make yourself come on my cock, ride me faster, *fuck me*."

I close my eyes as I feel heat rush down to my pussy, almost there—almost. When I open my eyes again though there's a movement by the door, and Killian is staring at me with his pants around his ankles and his cock in his hand. I glance down at Draven who now has his eyes closed, a grimace on his face like he's in pain, and it makes my stomach flip from excitement. I'm doing this to him.

To *them*.

I don't stop, and Draven reaches up to cup my breast and pinches my nipple. My hand slips and I wrap it around his throat, putting my weight on it to hold myself up. He grunts and turns red, but doesn't push me off him, but my eyes go to Killian. Silent as the night, fucking his fist harder. His lips are tight, his eyes on me as I circle my hips faster, and he looks jealous, like he wishes *he* was the one inside me.

My mouth opens on a moan, a loud one, and Killian's chest heaves as his own mouth mirrors mine. He's still so quiet, but his eyes say it all. If he got the chance, he would fuck me into the bed. Will I give it to him? Do I want to? I can't think like that, I'm with Draven. I will be his fucking wife. This is so wrong. But the way he strokes his cock so hard, so raw, so fucking tightly makes my breath catch in my throat, a gasp coming to my lips. It's enough to make me come.

I look down at Draven, who is now staring up at me, and I shift my other hand to his throat and squeeze as he groans and moans, his mouth gaping, his face turning a deep crimson color. He fists the pillow tighter, his knuckles red, and he begins to top from the bottom, chasing his release.

I look up again and make eye contact with Killian. Heat rushes down my spine and to my pussy, and I scream as I come apart on Draven's cock. Killian? He's fucking his hand faster, and right as I finish, he pulls his pants up and comes into them. His back hits the wall with a light thud and I grab Draven's face so he doesn't turn that way.

His hands come to my hips now, slamming me up and down on his cock until his moans crescendo. "That pussy is so pretty, Firefly." He moans, and I moan too at the words. "I'm going to come, and you're going to swallow every fucking drop with that tight little hole." I look up to find Killian gone, the door wide open. I plant my knees harder on the mattress and help Draven lift me up and down, going faster. His eyes roll to the back of his head. "Oh. Fuck. *More*." So I give him more. I bounce on his cock like it's the last time.

"That's a good fucking girl." I smile at his praise, my nails digging into his chest.

His face morphs into that of bliss, the one I've been wanting to capture in my mind forever. Eyes closed tightly, lips parted, a moan on his lips, and a frown on his brow. It's perfect, he is. His hips push up into me as his cock jerks inside me, and he groans as he comes deep within me. I fall onto his chest, my limbs spent, my body limp.

"That was amazing," he says softly. "*You* are."

"I'm tired," I reply sleepily. "Can I sleep on you?"

I feel his smile against my head. "Whenever you want to."

And that's how I drift off, on his chest, my ear to his heart. His cock inside of me. But the last thing I see before I close my eyes and let sleep take me under?

Killian's face as he comes.

I was warned by Draven that I'd be naked and uncomfortable, with my face painted as a skull, and blood from a girl on my arms. But he never said I'd be surrounded by *robed* people. That this is some kind of Halloween ritual, I'm assuming.

There are at least fifty of them standing in black robes, their faces covered, surrounding me and twelve more naked girls. We're in the middle of the woods, and there's nothing here except huge trees and a circle, and the girls are in it with me. The circle we're inside of has a star—or pentagram, as they called it—and it's carved into the dirt. There's also an eerie silence that has the hairs all over my body standing on end—as well as the chill in the air, it's cold as fuck. A group of thirteen men begins to walk toward us, all carrying a staff.

One of them pulls the robe hood down, revealing black hair and blue eyes, much like Killian's. In fact, they look almost the same with their straight noses and full lips. "Welcome to *Cinis*." The man with a booming voice begins. "I am your *Dux*, and tonight we will be giving back." Giving back? What the fuck does that even mean? "But we will also be adding one more person to the Family tonight. *One* of these women gets to live."

A chill runs down my spine at his words and a low chant begins, something in another language that I can't decipher. I look around at the other girls whose hands are bound and realize I'm the only one who is not, *again*. This isn't right. All these women that came with me on the plane look fine, well-fed even, but something just feels off—like there's evil in the air. An ominous feeling that has me tensing.

The twelve other men surrounding us have silver snakes on the back of their robes. I can only see them because of the way they're walking clockwise around the circle, chanting something low that I still can't decipher. One, two, three turns and they stop abruptly, tapping their staffs against the dirt.

The snakes immediately make me think of Killian's and Draven's tattoos, and I look around once more to see if I can recognize anyone, like Killian or Draven. *Any* familiar face would bring me comfort right about now.

Black robes, circle, pentagram...

That's all I can see.

There's fire everywhere. Four bonfires to be exact— one to the North, South, East, and West of the huge circle. And when I look at the crowd behind the twelve men guarding the circle, all of them are carrying torches. I want to know what they plan on doing with all this fire, but then again...I don't think I can handle it.

"I want to thank you all for coming to this retreat, and if you are not a newcomer, welcome back. We meet here every year for The Festival of Fire, to perform our ritual. *Cinis* has been happening for hundreds of years, and even two of the Presidents of the United States have been part of us. That being said, only those who belong in the Inner Circle will participate, but you are welcome to do as you please with each other." Something tells me that no good can come of tonight, and I will be witnessing something fucked up and depraved. "But we're going to start with the first ceremony, the most important one tonight, before we drink the blood and our inhibitions are compromised. Then we can all have some fun."

The *Dux* begins to rearrange the bound women around me until they're forming the entirety of the circle—lying down—and I'm in the middle, the robed men around us unmoving, not breaking the circle. There's one of them that overlaps though, inside the circle right in front of the rest, but I cannot see his face as his hood is up. I'm assuming it's Draven though.

I look at the man in front of me, *Dux*, now lowering his knife to a woman's forearm. "This ritual is a sacrifice —a show of power. We *are* the most powerful men in this country. And as you all know, the most effective sacrifice is that of a virgin, and the blood is the vehicle that we will reap from. Power. *Essence.*" He stops and looks straight at me, then slices the forearm of the girl in front of him, from wrist to elbow. She whimpers but doesn't move, clearly under the influence of something. I close my eyes for a beat and then open them again, tears trailing down my face. When I open my eyes though, he's going from woman to woman, slicing their wrists. Moans and whimpers filter through the air, and a sob threatens to claw its way up my throat. What the fuck did Draven get me into?

I look up at him and notice he's unmoving, his stance wide, seemingly relaxed. Bile rises but I swallow it down. Is this really the man I'm marrying? Has he done this before? Is he okay with this? My stomach contracts as a sickening feeling takes over my body, and I'm dizzy as I stand here in the middle of the pentagram.

Blood pours out of the girls' wounds, and as if the dug up pentagram is a channel, the blood all pools in the middle. Where I am. My feet are warm and sticky from the blood, and it gathers between my toes, which are now crimson-black. Nausea threatens to take me out, a gag taking over my body, and I breathe in slowly through my nose. Is this the marriage ceremony? What it consists of? What the fuck?

He takes the wrist of the very last girl and slices again, pushing up to stand. "I slay thee in the name and to the honor of the high and powerful being. Please accept this sacrifice and serve us faithfully, for better sacrifices are coming."

Then he looks at me again. "Kneel." The *Dux* commands, and when I look around and no one moves I realize it's because he's talking to me. I slowly lower myself, trying not to show anyone more of myself than necessary, but that just forces me and the blood to become more acquainted with each other. I gag again. "Hurry up, *pulchra*. They'll bleed out before we get to play with them."

At that, I feel everyone's eyes on me, and they're so quiet I can hear their erratic breathing. As if they're *excited* about this. My face burns as I finish getting to my knees and close my eyes again. I can't see this. God, help me. But I steel my spine anyway. Only a little bit longer and I'll be able to get out of here, I think. Draven never really explained what happens after the ceremony. If we get to just leave. It was a lengthy car drive to get here though, one in which I had to be blind-folded because I'm not part of the Inner Circle and women aren't allowed to know its location. It's a men-only show.

I try to control my breaths, willing the heaving of my chest to slow. It does me no good to feel out of control, to not be able to gather my wits in this situation. I need a clear head to be able to get through it, and with Draven I can get through anything.

Anything.

Right?

"Tonight we will seal the union between my son and his new wife, and we invite her into our Inner Circle. She will take place in *Sanguis*, the ceremony where she will offer herself up to her husband, blood and flesh. He will take his vows and she will become his, until death. This union will never be broken, as it is blessed by *Him*, and it is the most unholy of unions that He blesses."

I open my eyes to see the robed figure step up to the circle, walking toward the middle to meet me. *Draven.* My breath stutters in my chest and my heart begins to pound as I hear the squish of his footsteps in the blood. He then drops to his knees in front of me, his face still obscured by the robe.

My nostrils flare with fear, a coldness seeping into my bones. I don't want to do this. I don't think I can. I mean, their wrists are slit for fuck's sake. But what happens next? To them? To *me*?

"Breathe." A whisper, and I do. I take a deep breath that makes my chest expand and my heart slow down. "It's almost over."

I relax slightly, looking at the ground. There are two chalices and a knife, and suddenly my heart rate triples.

It was a terrible idea to look, and now I entirely regret being a snoop. But not really, because I'm going to have to have my eyes open for this. So I raise my chin and square my shoulders, not caring how scared I am.

"Look at me, baby girl."

I do, and my blood freezes in my chest, ice traveling through my veins and all the way to my dead heart.

No.

No.

"Kill—" I say and he pulls down his robe, a smirk playing on his lips.

"*Mea est nunc.*" he announces, loud enough for the entire cult to hear. "I claim her." His painted face is smug and possessive all at once. As if challenging anyone to say otherwise.

"You can't." I shake my head rapidly, as if that will convince him to retract his words. As if that will stop him from making this mistake. Draven will kill him and me. He will be devastated. *I* will be devastated. No, I cannot marry this stranger. I will *not.* "I don't want to. I want *Draven.*"

Killian gets closer, his lips flush to my ear, and my lashes flutter slightly as I breathe in his vanilla and leather scent. "I don't give a fuck what you want, Angel. As far as I'm concerned, all that matters is that *I* want *you.*"

"Please—" I look at his skeleton painted face as he pulls back—a match to mine. And as he opens his robe and drops it to the ground behind him, I notice he's naked underneath, blood painted all over his torso, an upside-down cross dangling from his neck.

"Athame," *Dux* says impatiently. "Knife."

I look down as Killian picks up the knife, his fingers around the beautiful crystal-encrusted hilt, and angles it toward me. Is he going to fucking kill me? And why is his dick hard?

My eyes meet his for a brief second and then back down at the three bars going through the underside of it. Is he... *pierced?* I meet his eyes again and he smiles smugly, looking down at himself and then back at me. My face heats as my gaze snatches on him again, unable to tear it away from him in something close to fascination. God, I need to get out more. I need to see the world. I can't be amazed by something as trivial as that.

"Hold your hand up, Angel," *Dux* says, and I do. "It's time to vow loyalty to your husband."

Loyalty.

What an odd word to choose for a betrayal. Clearly, he knows Draven is supposed to be here instead, and he's doing nothing about it. Where the fuck is he, anyway? Did he lie to me all along? Is this some kind of sick joke? Surely not, though. I'm kneeling in the blood of twelve fucking virgins. But I have no choice. Something tells me if I don't go through with this I will be killed, just like all these other girls will be. That much I do know.

Either way, I take a deep breath and wait for him to speak with my hand held up. I look around though, searching for Draven in the crowd, but come up empty-handed.

My eyes meet Killian's once more.

"Repeat after me," *Dux* begins, his voice booming

again, and I do, taking my vows. If only because I don't want to die tonight.

"I vow," my voice shakes in a moment of weakness, which I'm sure will only be followed by more, "to bind myself to you, from now until my death, and even after yours."

Killian slices across my palm, grabbing my hand and squeezing it until blood pours into a chalice. It stings and burns, and I gasp when he grips it tighter as he makes the blood flow faster. There's so much of it. Then he does the same to his, slicing across his palm and pouring his blood into a different chalice.

"With this blood," he dips two fingers into his chalice and runs them from my forehead to my cupid's bow, then from one cheek and over my lips to the other, forming an upside down cross on my face. "I anoint you and bind you unto me, blood of my blood, flesh of my flesh, until we join the gates of the eternal fire."

I freeze again as he holds up his chalice up for me to take, and he grabs mine with his other hand. He shoves it toward my left hand and tangles his arm with mine until my chalice is raised to his lips.

"*Drink!*" he commands, his voice rising. "And let us seal this bond between us."

Because I have no fucking choice, I raise the chalice to my lips and chug the thick metallic liquid until there's nothing left. I feel the stickiness of it dripping down my chin and onto my chest, and he drinks as well. I watch his throat roll as he watches me, and when my eyes find his again, the sapphire blue of his captivates me for a long moment before I force myself to look away. He sets his chalice down and so do I, then I stay still because I don't know what happens next. Killian grabs both my hands, smearing my blood with his, and then *Dux* speaks again.

"*Vinculum signatum*," he says, pride in his voice. "The bond is sealed," he clarifies for me. "And loyalty above all."

A man in a robe enters the circle, a brand in hand, and I tense. Is that...for me? Draven warned me this would happen, but knowing it and living it are two completely different things. I keep searching the crowd for him, as my body begins to vibrate. I'm shaking so hard my teeth chatter. But I look back at Killian and he looks so fucking...relaxed. Like this is just another day at work.

Calmly, the man steps up to me and stops right in front, kneeling and holding out the brand. "Give me your right hand."

I shake my head and Killian—my *husband* now—grabs my hand forcefully and grips it hard. A hot, blind-ing, searing pain flashes through my body as the brand connects with my hand, and I scream. Faintly, I hear everyone chanting "*vinculum signatum*" and I scream again.

"It's okay." Killian shushes me and lets go of my wrist as the robed man pulls back. "You're alright."

"No," I growl. "I'm not."

"It's not over yet, *wife*."

"Don't call me that—"

"Be quiet, brat." He shushes me again. "This is not the time." He looks down at my hand, the one with the slash, and grabs it. Directing it to his body, he wraps it around his hard dick. "Grab my cock, little demon. I want your blood all over it."

I do, my fingers wrapping around it and unable to meet each other, but I tell myself it's because I have no choice. *Again*.

He grips my hand and jerks it until my wrist is moving in an up-and-down motion, and I hold my breath as I feel him get impossibly larger in my fist. He moans as he directs the pace, and my stomach clenches as heat rushes south. My hand freaking burns, but I ignore it as I focus on his little whimper of pleasure.

"I'll tell you a secret, Angel," he whispers. "I'm expected to fuck you into the ground right now."

"No," I reply. "I will not have sex with you."

"Let's play a game, little demon. If I catch you, I fuck you." I clench my fist around his cock, the piercings hurting the gash on my palm. "I'll even give you a head start."

"Fuck. You." I growl. "The *fuck* you will."

"You're wasting time, baby girl." He growls, grabbing the back of my head with his free hand and tangling it in my hair. In one expert motion, he yanks my head back and makes me look up at him. My scalp stings, but with his heaving chest and dilated blue eyes it's truly the least of my worries. "You're mine now, Angel. Get it through your head. We are married. *Married*."

"We can't be." My voice breaks on the last word and I shake my head. "I'd be a traitor. He rescued me, he *loves* me."

"I'll never rescue you." He replies in a low, sinful

voice. "I'll ruin your fucking life and enjoy doing it. But loving you? I don't think I'm capable of it. I'll do you one better though. I'll be so fucking obsessed with you, I won't even be able to breathe." He gives me a long look. "Now let me fuck you so you can get me out of your system, little demon. I know you want this cock to fill you, to stretch you. The most forbidden things are the ones that feel the best."

"Kill—"

"What are you waiting for, little demon? *Run*."

I stare at him for a short moment until he arches his brow and grabs my arm, yanking me up even from his knees. He pushes me away from him, hard enough to make me stumble, and I look around. There's a tree line right outside of the circle, and if I run fast enough, maybe I'll escape him. Maybe I can get away from this place. Maybe just maybe I can find a way to convince him to let me go.

I doubt it but it doesn't hurt to try.

I look back—which is a terrible fucking idea—and see Killian standing at the edge of the circle right behind me, his chest only a few inches from my back, his cock almost on my ass. I peer around him and see the robed men kneeling next to the girls, drinking their fucking blood right from their wounds. Some of them are between their legs, raising robes and fucking them. I don't know how this ends, but I don't want to be here to witness it.

Dux's voice rises with each word. "We have one hour until *Cinis* is executed, and then the burning begins."

Burning? Are they burning them? Alive? Dead?

I don't want to know.

Making the decision quickly, I look back at Killian. "*Run*." He says again, and this time I do.

No longer looking back at him, I head straight for the tree line. The temperature is dropping and goosebumps line my body. Maybe it's because I'm slightly cold, or maybe my body temperature has to do with the sinister things happening right outside of these woods. It doesn't matter. I have to get the fuck out of here.

"One, two, Killian's coming for you!" He yells, and I pump my legs with all my strength, running as fast as I can.

It takes literally no time before my legs burn uncomfortably and my breath comes out in gasps. Fuck. Being in a basement for so long has definitely incapacitated me, but I refuse to look back and slow myself down.

"Three, four, you're going to beg for more!"

I focus on my breaths, in, out, out. In, out, out. Either way, rocks dig into my feet, sticks too, and I can feel my heels splitting open. It fucking hurts.

"Five, six, this is happening!"

Looking around, I see there's another clearing, and I intend to run straight across into the woods again. I could go through the woods still, but my feet could use the break the grass will give me. Maybe I'll even get lucky and be able to hide in a moment.

"Seven, eight, gonna fuck that face!"

But I should know better, I'm never lucky. Just look at my life right now. I was supposed to marry the love of my life, and instead, I'm married to his adoptive brother. His soulmate—whatever the fuck that means. Everything is so fucked up.

"Nine, ten, prepare to say amen!"

I'm tackled to the ground, my face in the grass, and a hard, heavy body blankets mine. His chest is to my back, his cock between my legs, and I can feel myself getting wet.

Killian is panting right against my ear, his chest heaving at the same pace as mine, and my breaths come out in quick bursts. His body is heavy and it's hard to breathe, but he doesn't get off me, doesn't give a shit as he crushes me.

"Caught you, little demon." He whispers against the shell of my ear, giving it one long lick. "Now hold onto the grass, the dirt, whatever you can reach. I'm going to teach you a little lesson on how to be properly fucked."

Killian gets off me, running his hand down my back, then grabs my hip and tilts my ass up in the air. I feel the wind hit my pussy, and a shiver runs down my spine at how cold I feel. But he doesn't seem to care about the state of my body as he runs a finger over my slit. So I do as he says, grabbing the grass, bracing myself for what's to come.

"You sure you don't want me?" He chuckles. "You're so fucking wet for me, baby girl. I might just drown in you."

"So *drown*," I reply with venom in my voice. "Maybe do me a favor and die."

"Such a feisty little thing, you are." He laughs, dipping two fingers into my pussy and curling them against my inner walls. "But your pussy wants me, and deep down you do too. You just think it's fucking wrong. *I* think nothing's ever felt more right."

Suddenly I'm empty again, except I hear rustling in the background and look over my shoulder. He's kneeling behind me, getting ready to fuck me. His piercings glisten in the moonlight, twinkling, blinding me, mocking my fate. I can't escape him, not with his newfound grip on my hip. Not with miles ahead of me. I'm not stupid enough to think I can outrun him, but I'm still going to try.

Soon enough I'll go back to Draven and we will figure this out. He will talk to his dad and we will annul this marriage. It's not valid, it was always supposed to be Draven. Killian can't just come in and fuck with that.

I kick back with my right leg, my foot connecting with his stomach, and he harrumphs. The breath whooshing from his lungs is satisfying, and I begin to get up. But he grabs me by the ankle as I'm pulling away, and drags me across the ground. My nipples chafe on the dirt, my skin screaming when the twigs and rocks scrape me, and I whimper.

"Don't be fucking stupid, baby girl." He growls as he mounts me again, his cock between my ass cheeks, his breath against my ear. "There's nothing you can do to escape me. *Nothing*." I breathe in deeply and buck my hips, attempting to get him off, and when that doesn't work I throw my head back and connect it with his nose. I hear a crunch and a groan, but he doesn't react other than that. Except his hips rocking against my ass. "I fucking love your violence, give me more, little demon."

I whimper at the nickname, loving it, but hating it all at once. "Get the fuck off me."

"No." He deadpans. "I'm going to ride this little body into the ground. Are you ready, little demon?"

"Never." I lie, but my pussy is fucking wet for him anyway, the fight making me more aroused than I care to admit. My pussy heats, all my blood going right to my clit, and I hold my breath.

"Ready or not, Angel. The Devil is here to claim that little ass and eat your soul." Even at my refusal, Killian pushes my face into the dirt, my nose breathing it in uncomfortably, and his cock nudges my entrance. I buck, trying to get free again, but he's crushing me. He slides in one inch, groaning behind me. "You're like a fucking virgin, little demon. If I hadn't seen you fucking Draven, I wouldn't know the difference." One more inch, and I moan instead, dirt getting in my mouth.

His piercings are rubbing against me, making me see stars. His huge cock stretches me, and it feels *so* good. I don't care about anything else anymore, not as the heat in my body rushes south and my clit begins to pulse harder, to the beat of my heart. "This is what I imagined all along, Angel. My cock filling you, stretching you so wide you'll be feeling me tomorrow."

With one long thrust he fills me, and this time we both gasp in unison.

"*So* fucking wet." He growls as he pulls back and snaps his hips forward, hard enough to jostle my entire body. "All fucking *mine*."

I whimper as he thrusts into me again, over and over,

hard and fast. I manage to turn my face sideways until my cheek is pressed to the ground instead of my nose, and I shudder all over. My pussy gushes with wetness, and my eyes roll back in my head when his hand reaches between us and he begins to rub my clit. I can't help but to rock back and forth, my traitorous body giving in to the sensations, the pleasure curling low.

"That's it, Angel." He groans. "I'll give you what you need."

"Harder." I moan.

Killian chuckles, "I'll hurt you enough in a second," he tells me as he pulls out, spreading my ass and spitting on it. I tense as his mouth descends on me and he licks in my ass, then spits on it again. "I'm taking the only virgin hole you have left, since I got robbed of the other one."

Instead of being gentle with my ass, he crowns me and begins to pump into me. Pain sears through me, feeling as he stretches me through the rim, and meets resistance. "Relax," he whispers. "I'll make this good for you."

I try, I really do. I know this is happening regardless, but the pain is debilitating as he goes past my ring of muscle, and I press my face to the dirt and grip it with my fingers as I scream. "It hurts, it hurts, it *hurts*, Killian."

"I *want* to hurt you, baby girl," he says softly, like a caress over my body. It feels so fucking right. But then he thrusts forward and fills me completely, and I eat the fucking dirt from how much it hurts. "I want you to think of my cock when your ass hurts tomorrow. *Only my cock.*"

"Ow, *Killian*." I gasp. "Please give me a second."

"Shut the fuck up and take this dick like a good girl." He goes faster, harder, and I feel his piercings rubbing me from the inside.

He begins to play with my clit again, and I press my cheek to the dirt once more as I close my eyes. Fuck, it doesn't hurt anymore, instead, the pleasure is coursing through my body and taking my breath away. I fuck him back, slapping my ass against his hips.

"Oh," I moan. "Like that, Kill. Just. Like. That."

I bet if I looked back, I'd be able to see the smug look on his face...Instead, his fingers pick up the pace on my clit and I fuck him faster, chasing my release. I never thought getting fucked in the ass would feel like this, like an out of body experience, but maybe it doesn't have to be bad with him.

He feels so fucking good.

"That's right, little demon." He groans. "I'm the one making you feel alive right now. No one else."

My spine begins to tingle, even more heat rushing south, and I grip the dirt until I know it's under my fingernails. Until they fucking hurt. "Oh, *God*."

"Look around, little demon," Killian taunts softly. "There's no God here. Only *me*." He fucks me harder, his fingers speeding up. "So call out to me. *Say my fucking name.*"

"Killian," I moan.

"Louder, baby girl," he demands with a growl. "Scream your lungs out for me. I want everyone to hear you, just in case they forget you belong to me now."

"Killian!" I scream as I begin to tremble, my legs giving out on me.

He holds me up with one hand on my hip, and continues to circle his fingers over my clit. "Fuck, this tight ass is doing things to me." He moans. "Come for me, show me how much you love how I'm fucking you."

I scream as the orgasm takes over my body, possessing me like a demon and gripping me with its claws. I bury my face and nails in the dirt again, unable to come up for air.

"Is that what you like?" he asks as I shake violently.

"*Fuck.*" I moan.

"You want me to talk to you like the dirty little whore that you are?"

My body melts into the earth as he removes his fingers from my pussy and grabs both my hips now, his fingers wet against my skin, and I moan again at how filthy this is.

"Yes, Kill. *Yes.*"

"Oh," he groans as I feel his cock pulse inside of me. "My perfect little demon. *Mine.*"

I start to believe it, that I'm his.

He's repeated it so much I think I'm beginning to be convinced.

"Say you're mine."

"*Yours,*" I say through gritted teeth, lying to him.

After all, I have his mark and his brand on the palms of my hands. But I'll be getting out of this somehow, I don't give a fuck how it happens.

CHAPTER FIVE

DRAVEN

The cabin is fancy with its wooden log walls and warm color palette. Hues of deep oranges and browns adorn every space, and they—The Fellowship—has arranged for this room to become a groom's suite to get ready in. Not that I'm looking forward to the ritual, but I do want to seal the union between Angel and I once and for all. I'm itching for her, ready to take her in front of everyone, claim her. Or if our dynamic is any indication, she will probably be the one claiming me. But I don't care as long as she's mine forever, officially.

Deep brown eyes meet mine as the girl mixes colors on a plate, the face paint taunting me, just a mockery of every time I've participated in Cinis—the ritual where we burn the virgins.

Pine Pinnacle—where our rituals happen—is the place where everyone dreams to go to. With its exclusive campgrounds and even more exclusive invitation, the all-male retreat is highly coveted. Not to mention what goes on while there. Today, on Halloween, is the sacrifice of the twelve virgins. Usually thirteen, but one of the girls is supposed to be sacrificed in a different way. To The Family—to me.

"*You ready?*" *A high-pitched voice asks me, grabbing the makeup in one hand, a brush in the other. The brunette with brown eyes is pretty, not my type, but still. Her upturned nose wrinkles as she looks down at the colors, and then she grimaces. I should be angry, outraged at her bravery, but instead I grimace too. I agree with her, this is fucked up. She works for us —an employee. And she's clearly scared as fuck. The poor mousy girl is always scared, and I wouldn't put it past our family to have her working here by force. She's pretty enough to guarantee she probably is.*

Her hands shake as they come right in front of my face, and the door swings open. I look into her eyes and nod, urging her on, when a deep voice that does things to me, interrupts.

"*Stop,*" *Killian orders, and as the leader of The Heathens, he holds power. The nameless girl steps back immediately, recognizing who he is. Goddamn it all to hell, I want to get this over with.* "*Leave us.*"

"*We're a little busy, Kill.*" *I huff, rolling my eyes. It's so like him to pull shit like this, but I don't cower. Just what is he trying to accomplish now? Is he trying to stop the wedding?* "*Can't you see that?*"

"*Leave us,*" *he orders again.* "*I want to speak with my little brother.*"

Little brother.

We haven't acted like brothers in a long time, haven't you noticed Kill?

The girl leaves without a word, taking the air with her. It feels like I'm suffocating, my breaths are stuck in my throat. He's wearing that stupid black robe with the snake on the hood. Thankfully I can see his face. His floppy black hair falls over his eyes, and he pushes it back. He looks boyish right now—yet I know better. He's the strongest of both of us, and that doesn't escape my notice. He spends hours in the gym every day. I do too, but he could best me any day. So I submit to him often.

Like right now.

Submitting.

Killian comes closer to me, shuffling his bare feet along the hardwood floors that match the logs on the walls, some kind of pine color. "Something has changed, baby brother." I narrow my eyes at him and he steps even closer, his forehead meeting mine, his nose brushing against my own. I don't move, stunned by the intimacy of it. This isn't what we do. Fuck? Yeah, we've done that before. But this... is different. "You see, I've spoken to Dux."

Not father.

Dux.

This is official business.

"And he has granted me something." He continues. "Angel."

"Don't lie," I say through narrowed eyes. "He'd never do that. He promised me—"

"Her?" He scoffs. "We share everything, Drav. It's what soulmates do. So let's share her."

"Never." I raise my chin at him, and this time he slips his hand around my neck, softly squeezing. My warning to stop being a fucking brat. "Not her."

"Never?" He laughs. "Then you leave me no choice."

My hands come around his neck and I squeeze hard. He squeezes back one-handed, unaffected until he starts turning red. "What the fuck does that mean?"

Men come flooding into the groom's suite, in expensive, un-creased suits. My father's goons. Killian's goons. My goons. But they don't seem to fucking care about me at the moment.

Killian pushes my chin up, making me look up at the ceiling, and my hands slip from his neck with the pain. His fingers pry my jaw at a pressure point, and my mouth immediately opens with the pain. I gasp when I feel something sharp at the side of my neck, my eyes turning blurry, white spots dancing like ballerinas across my vision. Slow, taunting, spinning. I fight back, but then I feel a prick on the side of my neck, a liquid entering my body, and he lets go of me abruptly.

I lunge for him as he steps back, a taunting smile on his face. "Sorry, baby." He grins as I try to get him, but just as I make it to him, I'm hauled back by the guards. "I'm keeping her. And daddy dearest approved, so no one will be looking for you."

I begin to buck against the guards, freeing my dominant arm and swinging at all of them, feeling my knuckles shift when my fist connects with a face. But not the face I want, no, that one stands across the room from me.

Continuing to fight, I release my other hand and fight back again. Now both my hands have connected with someone, my fist aching like it's broken. But I don't care, I do not fucking care! This cannot be happening.

She. Is. Mine.

The guards shuffle along and out of the room, pulling me high until my feet are dragging and I can't plant them on the floor. I know exactly where they're taking me—the fucking basement. Where people go to die. I fight some more, but my body begins to tire. I start to go limp, my limbs not functioning anymore. I feel heavy, and the last I see of Killian is him walking away from me—back to the groom's suite.

My traitorous eyes begin to close of their own accord, without my permission, and a cold gust of air meets my face as

*we descend the steps. They drop me on the floor, my head
bouncing slightly on the concrete, and I lie on my side.*

I'm so fucking tired—

The basement is dimly lit as I pace it, the drugs no
longer in my system. I don't know how long I've been
here, probably hours if I'm guessing correctly, and my
skin is itching to get the fuck out.

I scream, an anguished sound even to my ears, and
my throat hurts from the force of it. My heart thunders
in my ears as I see him fucking her in my mind, pleasuring her—*owning* her. Right in front of everyone. The
tears that fill my eyes are from the anger burning in my
veins though, there's nothing sad about them. Although
my heart still compresses in my chest and the tears that
clog my throat are bringing me pain.

My bare feet feel raw from the concrete rubbing
against them, and there are little blood stains left in my
wake. The betrayal riding on my back threatens to pin
me to the ground. I can't believe he drugged me, stuck a
needle in the side of my neck and knocked me out.
When I woke up, I was here. Locked in, no way out.

Fear should be dominating my body right now, especially with my claustrophobia, but instead all I feel is
rage. And that's all I want to focus on because if I think
of how I'm trapped in here with no knowledge of when
I'll get out...I might pass out.

I never told anyone about the basement—the one I
was trapped in with my girl. Not my dad, not Killian.
The only one who knows about it is Angel, and the only
reason my father knows about her is because I needed
her to be collected. I couldn't do it myself, they

would've never given her to me, and all that mattered was getting her out. My father doesn't particularly care about who I marry, and I told him I wanted her.

Only her.

Always her.

He gave me his blessing, but something tells me he blessed Killian too—just as he told me. After all, that's his son. He acts like I am too, but I know the truth.

The door opens as I pace the basement frantically, and my heart beats a little faster. Okay, that's a lie. A lot fucking faster. The drumming in my ears drowns everything out, I stumble but right myself quickly. I can barely hear the footsteps that echo as someone descends the steps. *Dux*, my father appears, his robe down and his bright blue eyes fixed on me. He scratches at his five o'clock shadow, and it pisses me off even further. He looks *just* like Killian.

He comes down and stops right at the bottom step, staring at me briefly before glancing around at the shitty conditions. This is not where people come to hang out, this is where people come to die. Then again, everywhere that concerns us is where people come to die, but the Black Cabin at Pine Pinnacle? This is where people come to either seek pleasure, give pleasure, or get sacrificed. Usually in that order. But the basement is frigid, the chains hanging from the ceiling taunting me, and the blood stains that will never come out tell a tale of what could very well be happening to me if I defied them on this. But I'd rather die than lose her.

"*Father*," I greet him through gritted teeth. "How did you find me? What the fuck has happened?"

"Well, for one, it looks like you've seen better days." He looks down my body to notice my torn clothes and bloody knuckles. Yeah, Killian may have drugged me, but it took multiple men to get me here. And I didn't go down without a fight. "And Killian confessed where you were. But I have bad news."

I already know the bad news, so I don't reply.

"You were nowhere to be found." He says as if he regrets what he's done. But I know better, he knew. So why the fuck is he lying? "Someone else took your place."

My blood boils, knowing the ceremony wasn't canceled. Not that I expected it to be, I know how shit works around here. Even still, I reply, "I know exactly who took my place. Killian drugged me and threw me in here. He took from me, and I won't stand for it. He said," I smile but it's not warm, a stiff feeling to my face, like the muscles don't want to work, "*you* sanctioned his union to *my* girl."

"Killian is your soulmate, what's his is *yours*—"

"Bullshit," I growl, and my nostrils flare with anger. "I want a council meeting. I demand it. And I want *you* out of it."

Silas is quiet for a long moment. He knows I have the right to this, especially after what just went down. Killian should've never intervened or tampered with my marriage ceremony. I want to know why he did it, why he got it in his head to marry *my* fucking girl.

"Very well." He agrees. "You deserve that much."

I've complied with everything he's ever demanded of me, so I agree. "Yes, I fucking do."

He takes steps forward until he comes toe to toe with me, and we're at eye level. "For what it's worth, I'm sorry." His voice is low. You weren't there, and the rules are the rules. Someone had to take your place."

"Get out," I say through gritted teeth, ready to lose my cool. "I want to see the council right fucking now."

"They're probably drunk on sex and blood." He smiles, and my hands itch to strangle him, throw him on the ground and beat him to a bloody pulp. I know I could do it; he's getting fucking old. "We just burned the virgins. The last thing they want right now is drama. But I'll make it happen, son."

The virgins.

It sickens me what they do, what I have to do every single year. Gather virgins and cut their wrists, drink their blood. The adrenochrome brings a high with it, an undeniable feeling of euphoria that anyone could become addicted to. But I don't want to think about that. I don't want to think about how they burn their bodies after fucking them. All over a show of *power.* Because they want to—because they *can.* Once they open the circle back up, a Samhain ritual, they come to take what's theirs in the middle of the circle. Fuck in their blood pooling into the pentagram. It's fucking *disgusting.*

I just now notice the stench of charred flesh on him, and I gag. My nostrils flare in an attempt to get the smell out of them, but it doesn't work. Instead I just take in more air. This yearly tradition always makes me want to throw up, but I've learned to play my part in every ritual, tried to be the golden boy who never disobeys. Just look where that's fucking gotten me. "I don't give a fuck about how drunk they are, Silas." I call him by his name, something I've never done before.

"You don't get to talk to me that way, insolent boy." Now he's angry. Good. "But I'll have them show up for you. They won't be happy about being interrupted though."

"Then maybe *I* shouldn't have been interrupted either."

Dux walks up the stairs and away from me without a backward glance, clearly pissed off by my disrespect. He leaves the door unlocked now. How nice of him. That being said, I have no intention of leaving this place until the council meeting takes place. I don't know how I'm going to make it happen, but Angel will be mine. She always has been, always will be. I don't care what she did, but thinking of Kill fucking her is making me sick to my stomach. She was supposed to stay *my* Angel, never his.

Does he hate me? Is this some kind of revenge for how I was forced to fuck him in one of the rituals? Yeah, we're fucked up, all our rituals are. But he seemed to be enjoying himself if the way he was fisting his cock and going insane were any indication. So maybe that's not it. Maybe it's jealousy? Maybe it's the way my father thinks that what's mine is my soulmate's as well? I don't know. But Firefly was the only thing I didn't want to share, and he couldn't let me have just this one.

No, instead he took her, marked her, branded her. All for *him*. I'll never be able to have that now. He took it from me by force. It's unforgivable. And the worst thing? Soulmates are forever. I can't even get rid of him.

I pace the basement for who knows how long before the council opens the door and shuffles down the stairs. My knuckles tighten at the sight of them, and I *feel* my neck and face flush. I can just bet I'm bright red with rage. But it's more than that, I feel my temples throbbing as the evidence of my anger takes over my body. My heart beating out of my chest.

I take a few steps back to put some space between us, needing it just in case I flip the fuck out. If the rage I'm feeling is any indication, the more space between us the better.

Men in black robes with silver snakes on the hood stand in front of me, forming a line, their faces obscured with how they lower them over their noses. But I know who they are, I've known them for years. The Fellowship is ingrained in my mind. I count them, noticing there's twelve of them instead of thirteen, and I relax slightly. My father did as I bade and didn't come. The twelve founding families left are my audience, but the *Dux* taking my father's place will have the last word.

"Explain." Samuel Rothschild says, my father's soulmate. Although his face is covered I can imagine his stern face right now. His blond hair. Deep blue eyes scrunching at the corners with anger for interrupting their little party. But his familiar features don't scare me anymore—it's been a while since anything has. Even though I have to admit he is a scary motherfucker with his rugged features, strong nose, and square jaw. His build is equally intimidating, and his height too, being about two inches taller than me, and I'm six-three.

They look pissed off that I took them away from their festivities. From the depraved shit they like to do. Or maybe it's over. Or they're drunk as fuck on blood and adrenochrome. I don't give a damn.

I want what's *mine*.

"I was supposed to marry Angel tonight, but Killian drugged me," I growl, beginning the painful confession. Painful because he betrayed me. He didn't care about us or what this might mean for our future. But I also feel anger, a rage that's uncontrollable in my chest, making me want to fucking detonate into a million pieces, blowing him up right with me. "Brought me to this basement, and took my wife for himself."

"She's *his* wife now, Draven." His face is serious, no trace of an expression judging from the bottom half of his hood. Except maybe an eye roll I can't see. "We both know that can't be undone, and there's nothing we or you can do about it."

"Yeah, *we live by the rules, we die by the rules,*" I say our motto through gritted teeth. "But what if I was betrayed? What if he's the one who fucked me into losing her? And he *did*. I brought her here. I bought her and bound her to me. She's *mine*."

"You bring up a fair point." He nods. "It is foul play, and for that, we will grant you one exception."

I relax slightly, until the door opens again and Killian strides down naked, covered in blood all the way down to his glistening cock—probably still wet with *her* —and his Jacob's Ladder piercing twinkling even in the dimly lit room. His torso is also covered in blood. I don't want to think about what went down with him and Angel, but if I had to guess, her hands were all over him.

Nausea threatens to take over, but I swallow it back. I will not show weakness in front of him. His face is placid, completely serious, and he seems at ease. I know he drank my girl's blood, and he's also satiated from fucking her. I don't give a fuck. I want to hear what they have to say, but I just can't stop staring at his skull face paint, all smeared and shit. A sign of the fun he had.

"You summoned me?" Killian smirks, coming down the stairs and standing next to me, his cock bobbing as he walks. He's still half-hard. I try to ignore it, but my eyes keep being drawn to it, down to the blood smeared all over it. The devil tattoo taunting me.

Fire consumes my veins as the urge to beat his fucking face in takes over my body, and I clench my fists until my bones grate and it feels like I'm going to pull a muscle. He's so nonchalant about this situation, as if he didn't just fuck me over. In fact, he turns his face toward me and smiles. My fists ache again remembering how I fought back, but I wasn't able to hit him. Now I *want to*. Maybe I'll even get away with it.

"Yes," Rothschild says, making the decisions. "We did. We're here to discuss the matter of Angel Murray."

"*Hansen*," Killian interjects with a grin.

"Hansen." The man affirms, further stoking my fire. He takes off his hood, finally, and looks at Killian with narrowed eyes, his lips set into a harsh line, his face tense. Disapproval written all over it, like a daddy scolding a naughty child. It's not enough. It will never be enough. "You will stand and face me when I speak to you." He says sternly, and Killian immediately complies, ever the perfect boy. Samuel continues. "Draven claims you drugged him, trapped him in this basement, and then took Angel for yourself." Killian shifts on his feet, seemingly uncomfortable.

I'm ready to hear him spit out lies at them, but instead he says, "It's true, I did all of that." That's more surprising than his betrayal, his candid response, like he's above our laws.

"Why?"

He shrugs. "Why not?" I clench my jaw with the renewed need to hit him. "I saw what I wanted, and I took it." He looks down at the floor, as if afraid of his answer for just a moment, but then I look at his spine, ramrod straight. "Besides, what's mine is his, what's his is mine, right?"

Wrong.

He and I are not fucking married, but in this cult, we may very well be. Being soulmates—it's the same thing. "No," I growl.

Rothschild nods, "Thank you for your honesty." A loud sigh comes from him. "But due to your admission, certain measures will be taken. We cannot undo your marriage, but we can give her free will." He raises his chin, then looks at the rest of the council. They all nod their approval.

I relax and Killian scoffs. "She's my fucking wife, she's bound to *me*. Fucking *mine*."

"She can pick whoever she wants to be with. She

was promised to Draven first, and you got in the way of that. You betrayed your soulmate. Either way, she belongs to *The Family* now. If she wants to act like a whore, she can. The Fellowship sanctions it."

I clench my fists and look at Killian, who also clenches his jaw at the word whore. At least he cares about that, because she's the furthest thing from one.

"She'll pick me," I affirm. "Angel always will. I'm the love of her life."

"We will see about that," Killian replies with a smile. "Now if you don't mind, I need to get back to *my wife*."

"*Fuck. You.*"

"Alright boys, I think we're done here." Rothschild adjusts his robe and turns on his heel, going up the steps with the rest of the council following behind. "Please don't kill each other."

Except I do want to kill him, but first I need to get Angel out of here. Away from him. I can't stand the thought of him touching her, and now I wonder if she liked it. Did he make her come? Did he show her pleasure or did he just take care of himself? I can't imagine her being okay with getting fucked in front of everyone. Is she traumatized? Did she cry? Was she scared?

Killian goes back up the stairs and leaves the door open this time, and I follow closely behind. He walks into one of the rooms where we are staying the night, and a lock engages as soon as he closes the door. So he *is* scared that I'll steal his wife from right under his nose, and I will. I'll convince her to move to my house, that was the plan all along.

I don't usually live at my father's house, but that was

his requirement until marriage. That she stay in his house, and I couldn't just leave her there alone. There's nowhere to hide though, not really. Killian is my neighbor, and the other four of the Heathens live on the same street.

Mortem Drive.

So either way it's not like I can hide her from him. She has to pick me. And she will, right? *She has to.* She can't possibly love him after one fucking night of what? A little pleasure?

But she's never been with anyone else but me.

Maybe it felt good to let go, to experience something new.

No, she'd never do that to me.

Ever.

CHAPTER SIX
ANGEL

There's a tingling between my legs as I rouse from deep sleep, and I groan, throwing an arm over my eyes. There's no light filtering into the room, and I wonder what time it is. Is it night? Day? I try to go back to sleep until there's a pressure against my center, and my eyes fly open with a moan on my lips.

"There she is," Killian whispers from between my legs. "That feel good, baby girl?"

Fuck.

His tongue spears my pussy, and the pad of his finger circles my clit. My legs come around his head, trapping him, and he chuckles against me. But shamelessly, I raise my hips. I remember last night—or was it *tonight?* —when he fucked me just like he promised. And I liked it. *Loved* it. I can still taste the dirt in my mouth, feel it under my fingernails, and more heat rushes south. He said he was going to ride me, and goddamn he did. I never thought I'd like someone fucking my ass, but it was a life-changing experience. Just thinking about it brings me to the brink—and now I'm flooding his mouth, my wetness dripping down to my ass, and he moans like he's the one being pleasured.

Two fingers enter me as he focuses his tongue on my clit now, and my fingers find his soft black hair, slightly wavy with some pretty curls here and there. I tug on it, loving the way it feels between my fingers, loving everything he's doing. Is this what lust feels like? Because if it is, then I'm feeling it. And I don't fucking like it. I feel like I'm betraying Draven, but it's not the same right? I'm married to this man. He's my fucking *husband*. Fuck, fuck, *fuck*.

Why is my body trembling the more he swirls and flicks his tongue over me? Why am I getting wetter? Why do I not stop him? Why am I being a traitor? *Again*.

Killian moans against my pussy as he increases the pace, his face moving against me, his lips wrapped around my clit. My toes curl and my back arches, making me tighten my fingers in his hair as his own curls faster inside of me. It feels so fucking good, so right, that my legs fall open as far as they go. He grabs one to push it toward the mattress and when he bites my clit and sucks it back into his mouth, I can't take it anymore.

With a loud moan, I come.

My body quakes, shakes, and it feels like my bones are about to snap from the pleasure of it. It's obvious he notices how much I liked it, because he hums as he trails his wet lips against the skin on my legs, hips, and abdomen.

He wastes no time, crawling over my body and

burying his face in my neck, his cock at my entrance. "You ready?" He whispers in my ear. "I want this little pussy wrapped around my cock."

My legs are still spread, and I don't push him away. "We can't, Killian. What if he hears? I can't do that to him."

"But *I* can."

"It feels wrong. I—" I swallow hard. "He loves me."

"He'll stop eventually."

"I won't." And I know it's the truth. I *love* Draven. "Ever."

"I don't care, little demon," he replies softly. "You'll love me too."

"I doubt that." I laugh.

He's quiet for a beat. In fact, I don't hear him breathe anymore. His body stills, tensing, and his breath whooshes out into my neck. Suddenly, I'm scared. I know I said the wrong thing. He's going to fucking kill me.

"Listen to me, Angel." He pulls back, his lips coming to mine and they brush against me in an almost kiss. "I'll tear your heart out with my fucking teeth and make you love me."

I gasp, my fear making me clench. "I—"

"Don't care," he says, licking my bottom lip, then my top, trying to get me to open up for him. "Give in, Angel. *Kiss* me." Tilting my head towards his, our lips brush again. "Give into me."

I can smell myself, and I breathe in deeply to remember this moment. Really immerse myself in it. He moans in satisfaction when I part my lips, taking my bottom one between his and sucking softly. He nips me as he lets go and I whimper, but before I can catch my breath he fucks my mouth with his tongue. It goes in and out, tangling with mine, and my head starts to spin. Bright white spots invade my eyes behind my closed lids, and this time I groan.

How am I lightheaded over a kiss when I'm lying down?

No one has ever kissed me this way, like their oxygen depends on mine slipping into him. Even if there's no chance that we'll ever be together—even if I don't want to—I know I need him right now.

I open my eyes as he pulls away, able to make out his silhouette as my eyes adjust to the darkness. Broad back, sculpted shoulders. Killer muscles that I can't make out but know are there. This man has an Adonis belt to die for, it's all I could look at after he fucked me into the dirt, the blood trail leading down to his cock. To the devil right above it. The light dusting of dark hair. *He's* to die for.

He turns me to the side and shoves a pillow under my hips, then turns me back. I know what he's doing, but am I ready? Can I do this? How guilty will I feel? How much more guilt can I take?

"Let me in, *please*." He begs, and I forget about everything. Right now, all I see is red. "*Please*." The blood from last night, my hand on his cock after he fucked my ass, how he fucked me *again*.

My bloody hands all over his chest and abs, the way I touched him and stroked him and the way he loved it—

I want *more*.

I vow to bind myself to you, from now until death, and even after yours.

Tilting my hips up, he gets the hint and positions himself against my entrance. "Always so warm and wet for me, Angel." I wrap my legs around him tightly and moan when he enters me slowly, then clench when he gasps in my ear. "You're gripping me so hard, baby girl."

"I can't—" I gasp as he enters me inch by inch. "It hurts."

"You're gonna fucking take me, Angel." He sinks in another inch. "You're gonna let me fuck you *so* good."

"*Yes.*" I moan again when he begins to move against me, thrusting in and out slowly, hitting a spot inside of me that feels impossible. "Kill—"

"Wait," he pants. "Don't say it like that yet, you're gonna make me come."

He pulls back slightly and when he slams back into me I see stars. "That feels so good," I gasp out, and he begins to move. "Right *there*."

Killian keeps repeating the motion, going slow but hard, his pelvis hitting me repeatedly, his balls slapping my ass. Obscene sounds fill the room, my wetness loud in the quiet between us save for his groans.

"You hear that, little demon?" He murmurs. "We sound so perfect together." With one more stroke of his cock deep within me, he gets on his knees and drags me closer to him.

His hands wrap around my calves and he puts my legs straight up to his shoulders, making my legs close tightly together. His hips slam against me—hard—and he moans the loudest I've heard from him yet.

"You like that, baby?" I ask him, panting, and he groans, "Because I do. Oh, *fuck*, I really do."

"Touch yourself for me," he commands, and my hand goes down to my clit immediately. I moan as I start circling it with two fingers. "I want to hear you come."

I run my fingers tighter and faster around my clit, closing my eyes as I feel the orgasm within reach. "Oh, God, I'm gonna come—"

And I do, clenching around him and spasming like I'm fucking have a seizure. It's weird, how hard he makes me come, like I'm pulling fucking muscles and I'm on the brink of death.

My breath stutters and I gasp, moaning again, groaning, making the most indecent sounds that have ever come from me. The sensation of him fucking me hard while my fingers are on my clit is enough to make me crest and fall hard, and he follows closely behind.

Killian lets my legs go and I wrap them around his waist, and within a few seconds he's burying his face in my neck and smelling me. He inhales deeply, groaning once more, and licks my neck then bites it hard.

This man is doing things to me I'm not comfortable with. I'm feeling something, I don't know what, but with every sound he makes, all I think about is how I'm going to make him do it again. What I can do to elicit those sounds from deep within him, to make him go fucking insane over me.

What is wrong with me?

He speeds up his thrusts, moaning into my neck again, "Fuck, *yes*." He groans, his movements sloppy, until I feel him come inside me. "*So* fucking good, baby girl."

God.

"I thought fucking your ass was heaven, Angel." He huffs. "But your pussy? It's fucking hell."

I laugh, low and throaty, and he chuckles against me. "Oh" is all I reply, because what do I even say to that?

"Promise me something," he demands. I tense, and he must feel it because his hands come to my face, cupping it. I can't look into his eyes, it's too dark, but it still feels like he can see right through me. "That you're mine now, and you won't ever let his cum fill you again. You're my fucking wife. Promise me."

"I can't." I shake my head, "I don't know what I'm doing—what I want, Killian."

"I don't give a fuck." He slides his hand to the back of my head and grips it tightly, yanking it back until my face is lifted to the ceiling, then he nips my bottom lip until a metallic taste fills my mouth. "From now on you'll think of me. Always of me."

The biggest problem is that he's right. I *will* think of him, even if I get Draven back. I'll never be able to forget last night and right now, I'll never escape him. I have a feeling this will haunt me, and so will Killian. But I know I can't stay, and he's hinting at knowing that too.

I can't stay.

I made a promise to Draven, and I didn't keep it. How can I be his forever if I belong to someone else? If

I'm tied and bound forever by a fucking vow? I really fucked up, or truly, Killian fucked us over.

"I promise I'll think of you always," I tell him, swallowing down the truth because it's a betrayal to Draven, but it is the truth now. Even if I hate this man for what he's done to me, I'll never forget how he's made me feel. "But that's the only promise I can keep."

"Are you fucking leaving me?"

I sigh, "If I have the choice, it'll never be you, Killian."

He flinches as if that hurts. But it can't hurt, not really, he must have known this was coming. He slid the rug from under my feet, he stole me from someone else. He fucking took me by force—just like everything else. He's a spoiled brat, and he sees me as a little toy to play with. When he gets bored he will give me back to Draven, and I'm not putting myself through that.

I have to hate him.

I *have* to.

"I'll have you if I want you," he growls in my ear, making shivers coast down my entire body.

I sigh, pushing him back, and surprisingly, he gets off me. "That's not how life works, Killian." I get out of bed and head for the bathroom, turning on the light. I need to get all this shit off me.

"No matter what you do," he chuckles, and I get goosebumps, "you will always be mine. Just look at your hands. The Family will not forget that."

"I don't know what that means, but I need to shower and talk to Draven."

Killian's jaw clenches, and he nods once. "Fine."

With that I close the door, not wanting to continue the conversation, and I get in the shower. The hot water beats on my back, and I close my eyes and sigh as I watch the blood drip down my body and toward the drain. The shower floor is pink from it, and it just brings me memories from last night.

From just now, too.

I'll be so fucking obsessed with you, I won't even be able to breathe.

My perfect little demon, so fucking mine.

Say you're mine.

The memories assault my mind and I try to ignore them, but it's useless. I have to get out of here somehow. I can't uphold this marriage. I need to get away from him as fast as possible. Draven is waiting for me somewhere, probably in another room, and he has more than likely listened in this morning. I won't keep doing this to him, no matter if I'm married or not.

Where will we go though? We can't stay close to Killian. I can't see him every day and look at the bond between us. I want to skin my hand and get the burned flesh right off. It fucking stings as the water touches it too, as if the universe is mocking me.

I get out of the shower with a clean face, clean hair, clean body. The only remnant of Killian is probably the cum inside my pussy. It still feels soaked no matter how much I wash it. Again, the universe reminding me I can't and won't ever escape him. If anything he said the other day is true, I'll never be able to escape this family again. I'll never be free and will always have to see him.

Wrapping a towel around my body, I leave the bathroom. I don't have any clothes in this room, so to Draven I go anyway. Killian is dressed now, sitting at the foot of the bed with the lights on, staring at me as I step out of the bathroom. His face is serious, his brows furrowed, his lips tipped down. A pang of sadness reverberates in my chest, but I ignore it.

I go to the door and pull it open, but before I can leave the room he says in a low voice, "I want you too, Angel. He may want you, but so do I."

Nodding once, I close the door behind me and go to Draven's room right next door. There's nothing else to say to Killian, not right now, instead there's plenty to say to Draven.

I'm so fucking sorry.

I'm a traitor.

I fucked him again.

I won't do it anymore.

Ever.

Draven is standing outside of the room next door before I can even think of what to say, and that's how I know he's been listening in. The pain on his face makes my lower lip tremble and my eyes water, and guilt eats at my insides all over again. He opens his arms and I run straight into them, sniffling into his bare chest, my tears falling hot and quick against him. His scent fills my nostrils, clean and something familiar, tobacco and cedar.

"It's not your fault, Firefly." He shushes me. "It's okay, we're okay."

I pull away and he takes me to another room, past the bedroom and into a living room. I'm assuming it's for privacy, because the walls might be paper thin. Fuck, he probably heard it all.

"I'm—" I sob as I fall onto the couch, landing on my butt and burying my face into a cushion. "So sorry. I'm so, so sorry. I'll never be able to make this up to you—"

"It's Killian's fault." His nostrils flare as he says the name. "There's nothing you could've done or they would have sacrificed you with the rest of the virgins."

My stomach drops as he confirms my suspicions. I wouldn't have lived. He has a point, but it doesn't make me feel any better. "Still, I feel like I betrayed you."

"Well, don't," he replies softly, his face a mask of sadness. "I spoke with the council."

"The what?"

"Focus, Angel." Draven sounds impatient for once, dropping to his knees in front of me, sliding between my legs and grabbing my hands. "They said you can pick who you want to be with, baby. That you can pick *me*."

I gasp, surprise filling me. They're letting me pick? "Really?"

Draven lets go of one of my hands and trails his up my body, where he holds it against my throat softly. "I love you, baby. You know it'll always be you. Will it always be me too?" He leans in until his lips are against mine, and he takes my bottom lip between his and nips it as he pulls away. "Is it me you're picking?"

"What kind of question is that, Drav?" I came here to tell him I love him, that I'll always choose him, and he thinks I'd choose Killian? Not in this life-time. "It's always been you, and it always will be." My throat feels like it's closing up, the mere thought of him feeling like I wouldn't pick him makes me want to slap him.

His eyes glisten with emotion, "God, I thought you'd stay with him out of some sense of loyalty."

"Loyalty?" I scoff. "Fuck. Him."

Draven laughs, "I don't care about anything that happened between you two, I know how it goes. I don't care about your marks, your fucking brands. You're *mine*." His hand tightens until I can't draw in breath, then loosens. "I want you and I always will. But we need to get out of this house."

"And where will we go?"

"You didn't really think we'd stay here?" He raises an eyebrow at me, letting go of my throat and sitting back on his haunches. "This place is only for rituals."

"I—didn't know what to think." I chuckle, looking around at the huge space around me. This place in the middle of the forest is at least thirty minutes away from the other house.

"I don't want to think of the ritual anymore," he replies. "I want to take you home, where you will be living with me, where you will sleep next to me every fucking night, no trace of Killian."

"Let's get out of here then."

"It won't be that simple," he says. "We will have to distract him, make him think everything is okay between us even if I want to literally kill him."

"Why?" I ask him, confused.

"The council meeting concluded that you can pick who you want to be with," he repeats, but my breath catches in my throat as images of Killian's hands on me come to the forefront of my mind, his lips on mine, his tongue in my mouth. How inconvenient—to have to think of my *not* choice. "But if you think that Killian is going to just let you go...well he's not."

"So how do we get home then?"

"Uh." He grimaces. "There's something I need to tell you." I open my mouth to reply and he raises a hand. "Please hear me out. The ritual you saw with the virgins...there's so much more than that happening throughout the year, baby. It's sick, it's disgusting, and I have no choice. I've never had one. If you want to be part of them, you have to belong. You live by the rules, you die by the rules. And they have a lot of them. When it comes to rituals...you can't back out and you can't say no. There's no consent, you just do as you're told. Sometimes, that involves sex."

I gasp. "You'll cheat on me?"

"Not in the way you think..." He looks away. "They think if we're...intimate...it'll bring us all closer together. Some of these rituals—well they drug us and lock us together in a room."

"So you and Killian?" I ask, and Draven nods, still not meeting my eyes. "Isn't that weird? He's your brother."

"He's my *adoptive* brother." Now he does look at me with an eye roll. "I met him when I was *nineteen*."

He has a point. They didn't grow up together, or that would just be fucking weird. "Do you like it?" I whisper the question.

"When I'm under the influence of drugs...well everything feels good, baby."

I grab his hand, my stomach clenching at what I think he's implying. "What are you trying to say, Drav?"

"That we should fuck him. Both of us."

"*What*? I'm not fucking him again, Draven." I huff, regardless of how much I want it, deep, deep down. "I won't go through that again."

"Oh, don't act like you didn't like it, baby." He says with a sad face, making me flinch. "I heard you this morning, moaning for him. I heard it all."

Fuck. I really have no way out of this one, because I can't even deny all the things Killian made me feel earlier. Wanted, worshiped, devoured. Will it ever be the same with Draven again? Will he look at me and hear the sound of me coming for his brother? I don't know, and it hurts.

My lower lip trembles again and I look away. "I'm sorry."

He ignores me, changing the subject. "There's clothes right there for you." He nods toward another sofa that has women's clothes on it. I look down at my towel and smile, knowing he's always taken care of me and always will. "All we have to do is get out of here."

"So let's do it." I say. "Right now."

"He will try to stop us." I know he will, especially after what he said before I left the room. I'm a bit scared at his possessiveness already.

"So, what?" I ask him, my voice rising. "Will we always be hiding after this? Am I going from one basement to another? I will not live in fear or captivity any longer, Draven."

"I don't want that for you either, Angel!" He yells,

"And once we're out of here we will be untouchable. *You* will."

"He knows I'm leaving him, I already told him I choose you."

"That won't stop him from trying to take you."

But how do I explain to him that I can't be intimate with Killian again? That hearing him whisper dirty nothings in my ear does something to me. More like undoes me. I can't make him understand, and it will be even worse if he knows it. But I can't pretend not to be responsive to him, it'll be impossible.

"Alright." I relent. "Let's get the fuck out of here."

But it's going to break me a little on the inside, because I don't know how to keep him out of my head. I don't think there will be a world in which I'll be able to forget him.

CHAPTER SEVEN

KILLIAN

There's a knock at the door just as I get out of the shower, my fluffy towel wrapped around my waist. It's probably Draven coming to beat my ass, but we both know he'll never accomplish that. Except when I open the door, there stands Angel in nothing but the same fucking towel she was wearing hours ago. Did she never put clothes on? Or did she spend all this time fucking Draven?

"What," I breathe in, my nostrils flaring with anger, "the actual fuck, Angel Hansen?"

"Murray."

"*Mine.*"

Angel huffs and rolls her eyes, pushing past me. "You are so fucking annoying. But I have a proposition."

I raise an eyebrow as I close the door. "And?"

"Draven is letting you fuck me goodbye."

"Oh, you're already back for more, little demon?" I get closer to her, taunting her. My hand finds the back of her neck and I pull her toward me until our lips are touching, brushing against each other. "Was this morning not enough for you, Angel?"

Angel tries to push away from me, but I tighten my hold. "Yes." She breathes against my lips, and her tongue brushes against them when she tries to wet her lips. "I'm back for more."

I rip her towel away from her body and drop it on the floor, mine following, and then push her against the wall. "It's a good thing I can't get enough of you."

This time she kisses me, her lips molding to mine, her tongue probing between my lips, and a frown takes over my face. Either way I let her in, let her tangle our tongues together the same way I want to tangle myself with her.

Angel pulls away, "On one condition."

Of fucking course there's strings attached. "What?" I ask through gritted teeth, my molars grinding.

"That he gets to join in."

"No." I shake my head adamantly. "I won't share you."

"You won't have to." She smiles. "He wants me to share *you*."

What the fuck? I know we do some crazy shit during rituals, it's expected of us. We're drugged out of our fucking minds and horny as fuck...but this? Willingly fuck him? Why now?

"I don't know about that, Angel—"

"Then no deal." She smiles as if it's nothing all over again, and pushes me away. Her ass sways as she walks to her towel and picks it up, all the while giving me her back, a prime view of her pussy from behind. Plump pussy lips, so fucking perfect. I can't just let her walk away. "See you later."

"Wait." I lick my lips, thinking about the implications of this. What is he going to do? What am I going to do? "I'm the one who gets to fuck you."

Angel shrugs, "Of course." I smile at that, "You're not sharing me, remember?"

She walks back toward me and I grab her arms gently. "I want you to fuck me like you fucked him, Angel." I lean in to whisper in her ear. "Remember when you were on top of him? Looking at me? Well, this time I'll be the center of your fucking universe."

With a loud gulp she nods and I turn off the lights. As she makes her way to the bed, I make sure the bathroom door is ajar for a little light to filter in. I want to see her face when my dick is inside of her, when I'm coaxing the deepest of moans from within her. I don't know what's gotten into me, but ever since she ran from me and made me chase her...I can't stop thinking about her, and I don't want to. I'm not stupid, I know what they're doing here. They want to distract me so they can get out of the house together. I'll entertain them because I want to fuck her again, but if he thinks he's going to be able to keep her from me, he's got another thing coming. The mere idea is laughable. No one takes anything from me, and apparently I've been feeling overly possessive of her since before I married her because look at me stealing her away from my fucking brother. I don't even want to think about what's wrong with that or me.

I look up to find Angel kneeling on the bed, waiting

for me. Her small tan nipples harden, her perky tits bouncing as she shifts her body slightly, and I'm transfixed by it all. By *her*.

Crawling across the bed and all the way to my pillow, I watch Angel's face as I do. She tries to not betray her emotions, her facial expressions staying mostly neutral. But I'm paying close attention, and I see the lust in her eyes before I'm even by her side. She wants to pretend this is all Draven's idea, that *he* will let me fuck her for the last time, but if she didn't want to she wouldn't be here.

I adjust my pillow and lie on my back, staring at the ceiling. Her breaths come out in pants, and I can see her chest heaving from the corner of my eye. But she doesn't move, doesn't even talk to me. Is she waiting for him to come in? *Fuck that.* I want my own moment with her.

"Get on my lap, Angel." The covers rustle a bit as she obliges, climbing on my lap, her wet pussy against my cock. What has her so wet all of a sudden? Is it fear? Does she like being scared? "Such a greedy whore, you are."

My fingers sink into her slit and I rub her clit softly, drawing a whimper from her lips that sounds like music to my ears. She likes to pretend that she doesn't like what I do, that I don't affect her in the slightest, but it's all a lie.

I curl my fingers against her walls, making her buck her hips, rubbing her clit against the palm of my hand. She's so fucking needy for me, and I love it. She's supposed to be the innocent girl that was locked up in a basement for half her life, but she knows what she's doing.

"Mmmmm," she moans, "Killian."

My stomach bottoms out at hearing my name on her lips, and this time I buck my hips. When I remove my fingers from her pussy, she cries out, making me groan.

I bring my fingers to my lips and suck on them, licking them clean. Her taste covers my tongue and I groan. "So fucking sweet, little demon. I would've never thought someone so feisty would taste this good."

My fingers come to the back of her neck and I pull her down until our lips meet, "Taste yourself on my tongue." She sticks her tongue out for me and I lick it. "So fucking hot, baby girl. You're ruining me."

A moan comes from her. "You've already ruined me." She scoffs. "You're the fucking devil."

"So sell your soul to me." I position my cock against her entrance but don't move yet. "I'm a little lonely, aren't you?"

"*Never.*" Angel whispers.

The door creaks as it opens, and I freeze when I see Draven coming in completely naked, a bottle of lube in his hand. He looks between us, pure jealousy on his face. But I don't know if he's jealous I'm about to fuck her, or if he's jealous she's about to fuck me. There's a big difference, and I'm hoping it's the latter.

Drav leans against the wall next to the door, and his cock slowly hardens. I lick my lips at the sight of him gripping the tip, then licking his finger to get the pre-cum off. My dick hardens even more, and I groan.

"Don't stop on my account," he says in a breathy

voice that brings butterflies to my stomach. The way he fists his cock and begins to jerk it makes me fucking desperate out of my mind for Angel to sit on my cock already. "Go on." He nods.

Angel looks at him, then me, and purses her lips. I'm sure she can tell there's something between us, more than what he's divulged. But she seems to not give a fuck as she begins to rub her wetness all over me.

Her hand reaches between us and she sinks down on my cock, whimpering. I know for a damn fact it's much bigger than Draven's, and that brings a sense of satisfaction coursing through my body. Not to mention, he's not pierced. I can make her feel things he never will be able to. In every sense of the word. I may not love her, may never, but she will fucking breathe for me if it's the last thing I do.

I look at him as she takes me slowly, inch by inch, and my mouth opens on a gasp. He's clearly affected by it as he looks only at me, the same face he makes when I'm fucking *him*. His eyes flare with uncontained lust, and I moan.

It's odd between Drav and I. We have a different type of relationship than brothers. Maybe I'm a little jealous of him, coming into my family after being an adult, trying to be the golden boy for daddy. Not for me, the one who's always wanted him. Maybe I should've told him instead of keeping it a secret, but I knew somehow I'd always be second choice to someone else, even if I didn't know who.

I look away from him, back to the goddess who's taking me way too slowly for my liking. "You're gonna take it, Angel." I grab her hips and slam her down onto my pelvis, impatiently refusing to wait for her to sink inch by inch. "You're gonna take my cock until you're so full of it you won't be able to fucking breathe anymore."

Angel gasps, pulling herself up and slowly sinking back down.

I shake my head, gripping her hips hard again and slamming her up and down on my cock, making her tits bounce, her breath escaping her in a whoosh. "Like. This."

"Oh, fuck," she cries out. "Killian, it's too much."

"Your pussy is so wet, little demon." Her muscles grip me, wet and tight, and I have to breathe in slowly to keep myself from caving into the pleasure. "So ready to be worshiped by me." She begins to moan with every bounce. "You want me to worship you, Angel?"

"*Killian*."

I grab her by the hair and yank her down, not directing her movements anymore, and she begins to move against me on her own. She rubs her clit all over my pelvis and lower abdomen, her wetness sticking to my skin, and I moan at how good she feels.

I moan in her ear and feel her clench against me, her pussy gripping me so tightly I see spots behind my closed lids. "Scream it, baby girl." I lick the shell of her ear then bite her earlobe. "Let him hear who you fucking belong to."

She shakes her head.

Slap.

I smack her ass and she whimpers, but she still doesn't do it. She rides me faster though, seeking her orgasm and making my head spin. I stick my finger in her ass and curl it, feeling her grip my finger so hard it's being pushed out.

"Killian! Fuck!"

I look over at Draven who's jacking off so fast his neck veins are bulging, but when he sees me looking, he squeezes the tip of his cock and stops, breathing hard. He *wants* me, he's the one who arranged this to fuck me. It's usually the other way around, but for him I'd do anything he wanted. I'll take anything he offers me.

"Don't come for me yet," I groan, trying not to come either. "Wait for him."

Nerves dance in my stomach at the thought of him fucking me outside of a ritual. Why am I so nervous? Why does this feel so forbidden? I've done it before, we both have. So why the fuck is this different? I guess it feels more intimate when it's done with someone else, or maybe it's because I can't hide how much I want it right now.

Draven comes to the bed and gets between my legs, grabbing them and spreading them for me. I hoist Angel up a little bit, keeping a possessive hand on her ass, and I hear the bottle of lube open up.

We usually fuck without it, just spitting on each other. Now I wonder how much better it will feel to be fucked with it, to feel him slipping in and out without resistance. Without pain. And getting fucked in the ass while my dick is getting fucked too? I don't think I'll ever be over it, and that won't be good for my mental health.

But I still spread my fucking legs for him because I want to experience it.

"You ready, Kill?" A forbidden whisper from Draven. "You gonna let me fuck this tight ass again?"

Fuuuck.

"Yes," I whimper, and Angel looks at me with a frown. That may be the weakest fucking thing I've ever done in front of her, but I don't give a fuck. I'm ready for this. I'm ready for *him*. I'm always ready for him. "Do it."

I feel the lube on my ass, cold and slippery. There's so much of it it's dripping down, and when he puts some on his cock and begins to pump it with his fist I harden even more inside of Angel. Painfully so.

He's looking between my ass and Angel's like he can't decide where to put his cock, and I growl. "In me." He grins at me. "*Now*."

Angel's eyes widen as Draven spreads my legs a little more, and she looks back to see him holding on to one of them. The head of his cock is against my ass, and images of me pinning him to the ground and fucking him come to mind. But this time I have the best of both worlds, and that's even better.

He pushes in slowly, and because I'm not used to it, it takes my breath away. There's pain as he makes it past my ring of muscle, and I cry out, tightening again.

"Relax, baby," he whispers. "Let me in."

I breathe in and unclench, and he slips in easily to the hilt. When he begins to move, I feel Angel grip me with her pussy. She leans down until her mouth is against my ear. "You like that?" She asks me. "Both of us fucking you?"

Angel moves against me, gripping my cock like she's suffocating it. Her clit rubs against me again, and my head begins to spin at the overload of sensations coursing through me. She's moving me in and out of her, seeking friction, and it feels so fucking good. But what Draven is doing? The way his cock thrusts in and out? It's making something painfully hot grow in my lower belly, through my whole fucking body. I'm hot and sweaty, ready to implode.

"Such a good fucking boy, taking my cock," Draven purrs, and my toes fucking curl. "Does my pretty boy like that, to be fucked and taken by both of us?"

I do, I *really* fucking do.

"More," I beg him. "Fuck me harder."

He does, he fucks me so hard I can hear and feel his balls slapping against me. The sound is so erotic that I have to ignore it in order not to come.

Angel starts to clench against me, her breathy moans in my ear driving me fucking crazy, and I know she's close to coming. Her hips speed up, seeking friction faster against her clit, and I stick my finger in her ass again.

"Let me suck on those perfect tits, baby girl." I tell her and with my free hand I grab one and direct it to my mouth.

Her nipple peaks more between my lips and I suck hard, biting down lightly. She moans even louder, "Yes!" She screams. "Like *that*."

I bite her harder this time, tasting blood, and she

begins to lose her rhythm. I moan when Draven speeds up and she grips my cock like she's trying to kill me. Heat rushes down my spine, down all the way to my balls, and when Draven starts massaging them my eyes roll to the back of my head.

"Oh, God, I'm so close,." Draven pants. "Come for me, Kill. Come in our girl."

"I'm right there, Draven." I cry out, and he massages my taint instead. My ass grips him tightly, and my hands grip Angel's hips. "Fuck, I'm so fucking close."

Angel kisses me, tongue and lips and teeth, and with one more rub of my taint, I'm shooting my load inside of her. I moan into her mouth, and Draven yanks her off me.

"Those are for *me*, Firefly. *I* did that to him." Draven moans, "Clench for me, baby. Make me come."

My heart speeds up in my chest at his words, bringing me joy. And I do, I clench for him, making his grip tighten on my legs. He moans and groans and then within seconds I feel him come inside of me. "Yes," I tell him, "give it all to me."

Draven pulls out slowly, then thrusts two fingers inside of me, making me clench all over again. "Such a fucking slut for me, Killian. You took me so fucking well," he murmurs, making my chest hurt, feeling like it's on fire. Draven is fucking worshipping me right now.

Goddamn.

I think I need a repeat.

He gets off me, and I lie down on my side and

pretend I'm tired, not wanting to see them leave me. Her leave me. *Him* too. And within a minute they've cleared the room, closing the door behind them.

But I'm not fucking done with Angel.

And this wasn't a peace offering.

I'm going to fucking keep her, she vowed her fucking life to me, and I'm going to *take* her.

Even what I feel for Draven won't stop me.

CHAPTER EIGHT
DRAVEN

I left Angel at home, sleeping in bed with her blonde hair covering *my* pillow like a halo. Not Killian's, *my* pillow, and nothing has made me happier in a very long time. We didn't stick around to see his reaction after we left the cabin, but if I had to guess he either lost his mind or was eerily calm. There's no in-between with him.

It's undeniable that it's been tense between Angel and I ever since we left Pine Pinnacle a week ago—she still couldn't understand why she had to be blindfolded —and she's acting like a jealous brat, too. I think it's because of what happened between us three, but she won't talk about it. Her lips are fucking sealed, and no matter what I do to try to coax the truth from her, she shuts down further. She has a problem with me fucking Killian. I know that's the issue. I just don't know how to fix it.

Which leads me to now, at Jagger Cargill's house, another member of The Heathens and my best friend. There's six of us total—all divided into pairs, soulmates.

And Jagger may not be my soulmate, but the friendship I have with him transcends what I have with the rest of them. What I have with Killian, on the other hand, is different and we all know it. It's not a friendship, it's not a sibling relationship, we're just...*more*. Soulmates, after all.

Jagger has been there for me since the first day I showed up. He took me under his wing and taught me the ropes, to live and die by the rules, to be loyal. To survive. If it weren't for him, I would've fucked this up a long time ago. It's how I became the golden boy—thanks to his help.

The morning sun streams in through the windows and I don't know what the fuck I'm doing here—why I'm not home with Angel. Probably because I can't stop thinking about how she's barely talking to me. How he fucked her and I fucked him. How that may have just ruined everything I built with her.

I think I really messed this all up.

Angel could barely look at me after that, and I know there's questions burning on the tip of her tongue but she's too afraid to ask them. Why did you do that? What is going on? Why did you decide to fuck him outside of the rituals?

I should be able to tell her more now, she's part of *The Family*, but I don't want to. I'm not her husband, so it's no longer my responsibility. Maybe it's fucked, but if we were married I'd keep her in the dark all the same. Killian on the other hand might be more willing to hand out more information, if only to get in her good graces. I don't know when he started getting so attached to her. Am I missing something? Was it when I asked him to watch her for one hour? One? Did they fuck before they got married? No, she would never do that. Up until now I was the only one to touch her, I should know that for a fact.

"Is this personal for Killian?" I ask the boys. "Does he have some kind of problem with me?"

"I don't think it's personal, Drav." Jagger says, his blue eyes rolling as he takes a hit of his joint. I snicker when he coughs and his delicate nose scrunches. He looks like a pretty boy with his dark hair and blue eyes. I guess I do too. But his square jaw gives him a bit more of a rugged edge. "Or maybe it is." He shrugs.

"Maybe." Asher Walton—another Heathen and Jagger's soulmate—hums from the other side of the living room. He's the brooding type—the silent one. Which is why I think it's odd for him to give his opinion. Him and Jagger are polar opposites. He's definitely the grumpy to Jagger's sunshine. "He might have been jealous."

"Of what?" I growl. "Not having me all to himself anymore?"

They both chuckle, and I close my eyes tightly, smelling the marijuana in the room and taking another hit of my own joint. Heat rushes through my body and I instantly relax, melting into the couch.

"Yeah." Jagger says, "Exactly that. He probably thought what's yours is his, and since you didn't feel like sharing, then neither does he."

"Did you talk to him about this?"

Asher cocks one blond eyebrow at Jagger and

chuckles, his crooked grin suddenly like a Cheshire Cat, straight white teeth gleaming, but doesn't say anything. I see him roll his light green eyes as my lips purse, and he looks away.

Instead, Jagger replies, "I may have."

"Well fucking enlighten me."

"I just did." He mocks.

How fucking convenient. So Killian did this to get back at me all along. For what? Not telling him about Firefly? Sometimes we keep our secrets, guard them with our lives, because it's all we have left of ourselves. Mine sure are. I've given every other piece of me to *The Family*, to the fucking Heathens. As my wife, I would've kept her as far from this as possible, unless absolutely necessary. It's not like The Fellowship brings their wives into their business and rituals. They keep them in the dark except for what they must know. It's a need-to-know basis.

"Fuck this shit." I sigh. "I'm going home."

I'm going home to Angel, to the love of my life. Truth is, I'm lucky as fuck to have her right now. The council could've said no, they could've denied my request, they could've not felt generous that night. The fact that they gave Angel the right to choose is astounding to me, even if they pissed me off by saying she could act like a whore if she wanted to. But she shouldn't have been forced into the marriage. My father was wrong for that one. I don't care about the damn rules, he should've never given Killian any kind of blessing. He should've looked for me before letting my soulmate have her. Or maybe that's the problem. The Fellowship firmly believes we share everything and that's why we're paired up. It's not uncommon for them to share wives. It's like soulmates are fucking married to each other too.

This cult is *fucked*.

And yet I know there's no way out of it. One day I'm going to finish law school and have a big fucking responsibility on my shoulders, a job of their choosing, and my life will be completely orchestrated by them. I'll be their puppet, and I know there's nothing I can do about them pulling my strings no matter how disgusted I am. As it stands, I'm going to be a judge in the Supreme Court of Virginia one day, then maybe even the federal government eventually. Everything depends on what they want and need from me.

"Can you even drive home?" Asher asks, but there's no concern in his voice, only a snicker.

"I walked here, dumbass." I retort. "I live two doors down."

The Heathens all live on Mortem Drive. It's a cul-de-sac that houses all of us. No spare houses. No one to know our damn business. And our parents and other influential politicians live in the rest of the neighborhood.

The District.

"Alright." Jagger says. "See ya."

I nod once and get off the couch, opening the front door as I take another hit of my joint. Except I come face to face with Killian, and I drop my weed on the floor and stomp on it. He has some fucking nerve smiling at me after what he ruined for me, what he *did* to me.

"Hey fucker!" Jagger yells at me. "Not on my fucking hardwood floors!"

"Shut up." I growl.

Grabbing Kill by the collar of his shirt, I punch him in the face. My fist connects with his temple and he rears back. I smile as I do it because damn it feels so fucking good to let the rage out, to finally be able to express it. I've been wanting to beat his ass since the basement, and now I finally get to do it. Not surprising me in the least, he immediately hits me back right in the mouth. Even though it hurts, I don't stumble, I hit him again.

This is for taking Angel.

And again.

This is for locking me up in the basement.

And again.

This is for making me want you and ruining everything.

He made me fucking want him, and now I can't get him out of my sick and twisted thoughts anymore. He's ruining my life in every way possible.

Jagger and Asher grab me by the shirt and pull me back.

"You motherfucker." I pant. "You thought you could just fucking steal her from me and we'd be okay?"

"Go inside." He tells the boys. "Close the fucking door. Let us deal with this."

"Fuck, no!" Asher yells. "Just look at you bitches, fighting over some girl you barely even know."

"Shut the fuck up—" I snap, and Killian says, "Go inside." At the same time.

I look back to see Jagger dragging Ash inside the house, whispering something and then slamming the door behind me. Killian takes three steps forward, caging me in with his forearms.

"You know how soulmates work, *baby*." Killian spits out with venom in his voice. "We. Share. Everything."

"Not her." I shake my head.

"Not anymore." He affirms. "I don't want to share my goddamn wife with you."

"She was supposed to be mine!" I roar. "You fucked that all up for me! How can you sleep at night?"

"With my A/C on sixty-nine and my covers over my head."

"This isn't a fucking joke, Killian," I snap, getting irritated. I can't fucking believe him right now, making light of the situation. This is possibly the worst thing that's ever happened to me. "You're breaking my fucking heart."

"You want me to fuck it better?" He mocks. "Want me to be your good boy again?"

"Shut the fuck—"

"Or do you want to do the fucking? I have to admit that was fucking good, Drav." He smirks. "I might even say the best sex I've ever had."

Heat creeps up my neck and to my face, remembering the shit I said to him a week ago. I don't know what the fuck got into me, talking to him like that. But I felt it in the moment, it just came out. It all felt so good, he did.

Such a good fucking boy, taking my cock.

Does my pretty boy like that?

Fucking hell, what have I done?

My dick hardens, pressing against the fly of my jeans painfully. He cups it with his hand, rubbing it with his palm, and I moan. "That's right, Drav. You liked fucking my ass more than her, didn't you?"

I wouldn't say more, but I'd say they're at the same fucking level, and that's a problem for me. I should've never done it, convinced Angel to participate in this fucked up thing between Killian and I. She didn't object when we were all in bed together, but now she won't even talk to me. Is she jealous because I fucked him? Or is she jealous because he liked it? Because he let me?

I open the front door to my house, the one I'll be sharing with Angel, and she just stomps on by me, not bothering to look back at me. This isn't at all how I wanted everything to go down. Not how I wanted to bring her home. But she's fucking pissed about the sex we just had with Killian an hour ago—the best sex of my life. I can't even deny that to myself, but I'll take it to my grave before I ever admit it to her.

"Angel!" I yell after her as she begins to ascend the stairs, "Please, wait!"

"Fuck that," she growls, spinning in place and holding on to the banister of the stairs. "One thing was fucking him to get out of there...and another was that."

"What do you mean?"

"You fucking loved it!" Her eyes glisten and I take a step closer to her. "You wanted him, you wanted him more than me!"

"I could never want anyone more than you." I whisper, the truth heavy between us. "Baby it's us forever, remember?"

"I saw it in your eyes, Draven." She spits. "I saw how you looked at him! You couldn't get enough! You wanted more."

I look down at the ground and clasp my hands together, then look up at the hurt in her eyes—the one I don't want to see. The one that breaks my heart. The worst part is that she's right. "We're different—him and I." I breathe in slowly. "It's been years just him and I. He has staked his claim on me, baby. But I swear it—I'll get me back."

"I was already supposed to have you back."

"No, I didn't like fucking you better." I growl and push him back, but he doesn't stumble like I hoped. "We will never be okay again, Kill. *Never.* I won't fucking forgive this. I'll do my job and you'll do yours, but trust me when I say my cock will never be inside you again."

"Drav." He tuts, his face a mask of arrogance. Fire fills my chest as I try to restrain myself from hitting him again. "Next time it'll be me fucking that pretty ass."

I roll my eyes, knowing damn well that he could be right. I'm weak, I always have been. While we never fucked outside of rituals, doing it was the only thing I looked forward to when we had to. But I'll never admit that to him.

"Never again, Killian."

"The Fellowship will never deny me the right to enforce my marriage, Draven. You'd do well to remember that."

A chill runs down my spine at his words and I push past him, bumping him with my shoulder. We're the same height, maybe he's a little taller than me at six-four, but he doesn't even fucking budge. Instead he winks at me and opens the front door of the house, slipping in and leaving me alone on the sidewalk.

I planned to just walk aimlessly for a while, but instead I head home, knowing I have to face Angel at some point. It's getting later in the morning, and I left her all alone in the house without even acknowledging her existence. She was asleep, but still, it feels wrong of me to have done it.

My feet are heavy as I force myself to walk home, feeling rage with Killian and sadness with Angel. I don't want to fight with her, it's been a fucking week, but I know it's coming—and it makes it even harder to go home. I don't know how I'm going to fix this, but I need to. *Somehow* I need to.

My hand wraps around the doorknob, and it turns easily when I try to open it. I could've sworn I locked it on my way out. With a frown on my face, I slip in quietly to see Angel sitting on the couch, watching tv in the living room. She doesn't even look at me when I slam the door behind me, and that fucking bothers me.

"The door was unlocked when I came in, Angel." I call out softly, "Is everything okay?" I know nothing is okay, but I also don't want her to be unsafe. Or did Killian come see her before going to Jagger's house? Is that why the door is unlocked?

Silence.

She's completely ignoring me.

I go to the living room and grab the remote, turning off the television and slipping it into my back pocket.

She doesn't react, doesn't reach out, doesn't even fucking look at me.

"Angel." I growl. "Look at me." My hands tremble, my body responding to the simmering anger I feel toward her. I think this is enough, this little ruse she's putting up. At some point she has to give this up—has to move on from it if we're going to be together.

But she still doesn't look at me.

"Fucking. Look. At. Me." Her blue eyes meet mine, finally. Her lips are pursed, her body tense. I want to take it all away. I want her back. *My Firefly*. "What the hell is your problem?"

"*You*." She tells me with a whisper. "You fucking betrayed me."

"*Betrayed* you?" I ask, outraged. "I got you out of there, Angel! He would've never let you go!"

"He did, though!" She screams, and I'm so taken aback that I take a step forward out of instinct. Fight or flight. *Fight*. My hands ball into fists until my short nails draw blood on the palms of my hands. "He was awake! He was going to let me go anyway!"

"Bullshit! He let us go because I appeased him!" I yell. "I gave him a part of me he fucking wanted, and he let us go."

"He is your *brother*." She deadpans, looking disgusted. It bothers me, for some reason the accusation feels worse than it should. Angel is making me sound dirty, like I'm tainted. I bet the little voices in her head she told me about long ago are wrestling with that comment, her face shows it. It's as if she's torn with that nagging thought of him and I. But he's not my fucking brother. I don't care if she thinks it.

"*Adoptive* brother." I clarify. "When I met him, I was already an adult."

"Doesn't this feel wrong?" She asks me, her eyes tearing up. "It should feel wrong to fuck him."

Yes.

No.

"Did it feel wrong to have his cock inside you instead of mine?" She looks away, giving me my answer. "You didn't even hesitate, Angel."

"He's my—"

"Don't fucking say that shit to me." I roar, taking a step back and throwing the remote against the wall. She yelps as it falls broken to the hardwood floor. "We are forever. What you have with Killian is a fucking mistake."

"Okay." She breathes softly. "You and I—you're right. We have always been forever. But Drav...this can't happen again. I can't have sex with him again."

"Why?" I frown. Not that I want to share her in the first place. "Are you scared you're gonna catch feelings or something?"

Her hands twist in her lap and she doesn't look at me. I knew it. I knew there was something wrong. Of course she could feel something for him, she's never been with anyone else but us, no matter how forced her marriage has been.

I walk up to her and kneel between her legs, spreading them wider apart to fit. "Angel." I brush my knuckles across her cheek and she gasps when she looks at my mouth. I think this is the first time she's looked at me since we came in the house, and her eyes well up with fresh tears. "Do you feel something for him?"

"What happened to you?"

I sigh, retracting my hand and searching her eyes. "Do you feel something for him?"

"*Hate.*" She lifts her chin and squares her shoulders. "And I never want to see him again, but I know now that I'll have to."

"Oh?" She's not wrong, but did Killian say something? "How do you know?"

"I'm not fucking stupid, Draven." Her hand comes to my face and she cups one cheek. "Stop keeping me in the dark."

"You're right," I tell her. "We will be seeing him again. It's inevitable with us being soulmates, we will have to work together."

"Doing what?" She asks, but I shake my head with a non-answer. I can't divulge the jobs we do. Not to mention the shame I feel. Being in charge of weapons distribution and trades, drugs, the black market. Human trafficking with the cartel. "What about Killian? Will he respect my decision?"

"Angel." I close my eyes and lean in until my forehead meets hers. "If Killian wants to take you and enforce your marriage...there's nothing I can do. The Fellowship will approve. "

My eyes flash open and I see the pain on her face, but also so many questions flitting through it. "So what now?"

"We *hope* that Killian respects this, because if not... I'll fucking kill him myself."

"*Kill* him?" She squeaks out. "You'd do that?"

"I'd do anything for you."

And I mean that. I'd kill, maim, run away. Anything to keep her. The thing is, I have a feeling Killian would do the same too. Not because he loves her, but to prove a point.

Fuck him for that.

She's not a fucking toy, and I'm not playing this damn game with him.

CHAPTER NINE
ANGEL

The conversation I had with Draven yesterday pissed me off even more than I already was. Part of me feels that he's right about Killian letting us go because he appeased him, but it doesn't make me less pissed off. I could see it in Killian's eyes that he wanted us both, but the way he was vulnerable for Draven... whimpering and looking at him with crumbling walls made me understand that this reaches far beyond me. There's something between them that they don't want me to understand, and Draven can say whatever he wants but I'm not stupid. I *know*. I can feel it. He wants Killian the same way Killian wants him, and I don't know that I can compete. Not when they know things about each other that I never will. But I don't see myself having many options considering my circumstances, and I'd rather be with him than Killian.

Fuck my life.

I need to find a way out of this.

My only entertainment so far has been looking up recipes and attempting to make them. They have all failed because I don't remember much about being in a kitchen. It's been a very long time since I even attempted to cook before this, but even though I know I should stick to sandwiches until Drav explains how to do this shit, I still find myself grabbing pancake mix and a pan. This is the one thing I remember how to cook, and maybe with some practice I won't mess them up. If I'm lucky, they will be edible...enough.

I've already preheated the pan and put the mix into a glass container, all that's left is water according to the instructions. I grab a measuring cup and fill it with tap water, then dump it into the mix and start stirring, knocking mix onto the counter with the force of it.

I try to breathe in slowly through my nose, trying to cool the fire inside of me, but no matter how much I try to use coping skills, I cannot fucking achieve it. I just want to break everything and go back to the basement. I want to be that girl again—the one who idolized Draven before everything went to shit.

Remember, no clumps.

I stir the batter some more until there's no clumps and it's slightly bubbling. This is the only meal I made with my mother before she died, which is when I was seven. I was adopted by my new family when I was nine, but the truth is I never belonged, and they knew it. Shit, I knew it before they did. I was never going to be what they wanted, and I was so scared they would give me back that I tried so hard for them. Until I couldn't anymore.

My adoptive parents soon realized I'd never be religious like them, that even the thought of learning about their God was repulsive to me. My mother had never forced it upon me, but these people made me breathe Bible verses as if my life depended on it. I still managed to get a few things I wanted though, even from that fucking basement. One of my sisters came down every once in a while and talked to me. She wasn't exactly what she pretended to be, and she told me all about her boyfriends, the drugs she was using, and she cussed a lot when she talked. I guess I learned a thing or two from her, especially when she brought beer with her and... other things. Kim didn't come often enough though, and if she were ever caught she would've never admitted to why she was down there: because we were friends. At least I thought so, until she stopped coming too.

And that's my biggest fear when it comes to Draven. Will he leave me too? Will he tire of the games with Killian and hand me over?

I'd fucking kill him.

Stab him.

Shoot him.

Fucking smother him.

I don't care. I don't care.

I don't care—At least that's what I'm trying to tell the voices in my head, trying to convince them. But even they know it's not true.

I'm supposed to be his favorite person, the one he confides in, the one he trusts. But apparently that's Killian. I know Draven is keeping secrets, and he doesn't want to fucking give them to me. He won't offer them up as readily as Killian, and curiosity killed the cat. I'm the damn cat, and I want answers. Now that's a huge problem for me because I want nothing to do with my—*husband*. But here I am sticking my nose where it doesn't belong and demanding that they feed me information. Except I was told when I became part of *The Family*, I would know more.

And so far I know nothing more.

Nothing.

I take a ladle to the batter and fill it up, then after spraying the pan I drop it in. It's not a perfect circle, but it's good enough for me. Drav will probably laugh at me about it, but I don't care. I'd say it's a pretty fair first attempt. He told me I didn't need to do this—cook—that someone would come every day and bring fresh meals for us. But I feel useless, like I don't know how to do anything for myself, and I need to learn how. What if one day I don't have him to fall back on? What if one day I disappear and leave them behind so I don't have to deal with this anymore?

Run away.

Fucking leave him.

Kill them all.

Shut the fuck *up!*

I don't even know what The Family does, the hierarchy—because it's obvious they have one—the virgins being sacrificed and then burned. Yeah, what the fuck is that all about? Why would they do that? It's clear to me they're not honest people, that they're evil, and Drav mentioned he has no choice. But what else has he done for them? What does he put his soul on the line for? I don't want to think about it, but it feels like there's something illegal happening. I mean, obviously. These people are fucking murderers. But is Draven? Is Killian? Did I fuck two killers? Will they kill *me*?

No.

You can kill them first.

Goddamn it. Shut *up*.

I pull my hair, hurting my head, ripping some strands. I guess it's a good thing my hair is thick. I'm so fucking tired of the voices that taunt me. They won't shut up. But they're right. They're right. And I can't even ignore them anymore.

Sliding down to the hardwood floor against the island cabinets, I leave the pancake unattended. Fuck, I hate doubting him. I *really* hate it. But Draven would never do that to me. I'm his *Firefly*. I'm the love of his life and he came after me, rescued me, when he didn't have to. He could've moved on with his life and married someone his family approved of, but he chose me. Now it's my turn to choose him no matter how scared I am to do so. I just need more answers, that's all. I need to know what they've gotten me into, because even I know this wasn't my doing. I didn't fucking choose this!

I get up from the ground and flip the pancake, waiting for it to be golden on the opposite side, then I put it on a plate. Just as I fill the ladle once more, I hear footsteps coming down the stairs. I don't put the batter in the pan, instead I hold my breath the whole time until Draven enters the kitchen, then I let it out slowly, turning off the burner.

Don't kill him.

You're fucking pissed.

Don't do it.

You love him.

My heart beats loudly in my ears, thundering, and I wonder if he can tell I'm nervous right now. I don't even know why I am though, I just want answers. I want to stop being kept in the dark, feeling unimportant. He's made me feel nothing but loved in the past, but then again he's keeping secrets. He's not giving himself to me.

"'Morning." Draven says, his voice deep and hoarse from sleep. "You're making pancakes, baby?"

I turn around and look at him, letting my eyes roam appreciatively down his body. He's shirtless, his chiseled chest and abs on display, and gray sweats slung low on his hips. He smiles when my gaze lingers on his dick, and my eyes snap back up to his. *No.* I'm still pissed at him, so I narrow my eyes and purse my lips.

"It's the only thing I know how to make." I reply with an attitude, my voice taking on an edge of anger. But still, I offer him the plate. Should've fucking poisoned it.

No.

"Do you want this one? It's warm."

I push the plate toward him on the island, and he smiles coquettishly. "The only thing I want for break-fast is *you*." Draven suggestively grabs himself through his sweats, and images of us in that basement flood back into my brain. It's easy to forget everything when he's around, to get lost in him. "Take off your shorts."

"Make me." I growl. "Because I'm not *giving* you shit."

But still, my panties dampen immediately at his

command, and some sick part of me wants to be fucked against this damn island so hard there will be bruises tomorrow. Just so I don't have to remember Killian fucking me. I need something to distract me from him calling me his damn whore, because after he fucked me with Draven...I definitely feel like one. I'm also not sure I want his dick inside of me after what he did to me, the way he fucked Killian. He doesn't love me, he loves *him*. He doesn't want me, he wants *him*. Draven doesn't deserve my pussy, so if he wants it, he's going to have to take it.

Draven walks up to me, abandoning the pancake, and yanks my hair back. My pussy floods, desire curling through my body. The heat that fills my lower belly is uncomfortable, and when he takes off my shorts and underwear one handedly, dropping them to the ground and pressing me against the counter, I suppress a whimper.

Don't show weakness.

"Hands on the island counter and arch your back for me, baby."

"No." I growl. "*No.*"

"You want me to make you, Firefly?" He asks against my ear, his tongue poking out to lick the shell of it. "You want me to act like him? Fuck you like him? What happened to my girl? The one who takes *me* instead?"

"The only way you're fucking me is if you take it, Draven." I reply as he pushes my hips into the counter. "Because right now? I don't even want to see your face, damn it!" My yell echoes in the kitchen, filling my ears over and over.

I don't even want to see your face.
I don't even want to see your face.
I don't even want to see your face.

"You're a little fucking liar." He growls, arching my back with one bruising hand on my hip, pushing my ass toward him. His fingers come between my ass cheeks and toward my pussy, and he inserts two of them in. I cry out when he begins to curl them inside of me, and I'm a panting mess within two strokes. He *really* knows how to do that. "I want you, baby. I don't want *him*. Who's here with me? Who sleeps in my fucking bed every night? If I wanted it to be him, I could have him."

"So you're saying he wants *you*?"

"It doesn't matter what he wants, Angel. He *took* something from me," Draven says softly, his cock against my ass as he works his fingers between my legs. "And I want it back."

"What, Drav?" I ask him with a shaky voice, my head spinning as I try to figure out what it is that he wants. "What did he take?"

Draven inserts one more finger into my pussy and I gasp, then he drops to his knees behind me and spreads me with his free hand. His tongue comes to my puckered hole as he thrusts his fingers in and out, and my eyes roll back.

"*You,*" he breathes against my ass. "Give yourself to me. I'll fuck you right, Angel."

"Take it." I growl, feeling my body heat up, butterflies filling my lower belly.

"This ass is mine, baby." His fingers disappear from my pussy as he gets up from the ground, pressing his hard cock against me. He brings his hand to my face, smearing my wetness across my cheek. It's fucking filthy, and it only makes me get wetter. "Grip the counter harder, *Firefly*, this one will hurt."

I grip the counter and look back at him, watching him drop his sweats to the ground and stroke his cock. Just as I think he's going to fuck my ass though, he directs himself into my pussy and slams in. I moan and drop my face to the counter, my cheek on the cold surface, my eyes zeroed in on the knives right next to me, and he pulls back and slams back in. My pussy burns as my hips slap repeatedly against the cabinets, rocking my entire body, surely bruising me. The pain grounds me though, and when I cry out, it's from pleasure.

His knees bend to try to get to my height, but he's too tall. Instead, he holds my hips and lifts me toward him, pulling me away from the edge. "I'm just getting you ready, baby," he whispers between a moan. "I'm fucking that ass if it's the last thing I do."

"*Do* it." I remember how he fucked Killian's ass, how Killian fucked mine, and I *want* him to hurt me. Dirty me up. I want to see the aftermath of his bullshit. I want him to hurt me so bad that I want to hurt him even more than I already do. "Pull out of me and fuck my ass then. I want to see the bruises on my hips as a reminder of the pain you've put me through. Fuck me harder than the way I want to fucking slap you right now."

"Oh, you want me to fuck you hard?" Yes. *Yes*. "Are

you going to be a slut for me too?" He groans, "Just like Kill?"

I freeze, but he doesn't even care as he pulls out and sets me on the island, pulling me down until the cold countertop meets my back and makes me shiver. My lower half hangs off it, making it easier for him to fuck me.

Draven spreads my cheeks again, spitting on me, then shoving himself back into my pussy. "You're gonna feel so fucking good, baby." He moans as he sneaks a hand between us and rubs my clit slowly. "My cock is so wet with you, it's gonna slip right in."

Draven pulls out of my pussy and shoves himself inside my ass, *hard*. He has no mercy, gives me no reprieve as he pushes past the ring of muscle and forces himself to the hilt. "Oh, fuck." I yell through the pain.

He moves against me, thrusting in and out roughly, picking up the pace until my back is slapping against the counter painfully, surely leaving those bruises I've been begging for. It burns so bad, but he's not wrong, his dick is so wet it slides easily.

"Your first time was supposed to be with *me*," Drav growls, pulling back and slamming back in. My hands try to grip the counter, but it's useless. They're sweaty and slipping. "It belonged to me. *You* belong to *me*."

He pulls out and flips me over onto my belly, then thrusts right back into my ass. "Now be a good girl and play with your pretty pussy." I moan as my hand goes down between my legs, caught between the counter, feeling like it's going to fucking break from his pace. "I want to see my cock stretch your ass, Firefly."

I hook two fingers in and rub my clit with the palm of my hand, all while his hips now hit the counter repeatedly. Heat rushes my body, making my legs tingle, and I rub faster, finger myself harder.

"I'm never gonna get enough, baby." Draven moans as my fingers speed up, my palm too, I'm right *there*. "I'm gonna come soon baby, I need to go harder. This tight hole is ruining my fucking life."

"Oh, God, it feels so good, Drav." I moan as I feel myself stretching, "Draven right there, *don't* stop."

My body begins to spasm, my legs shaking and opening wider, and he fucks me harder than he ever has before. "Look at you coming all over my cock, baby. Such a good fucking girl for me."

I scream, not able to hold back anymore and he moans as we come together, making my stomach flip. The thing with him is that it's not only lust between us, I actually love him. He gives me butterflies with every sound he makes, and I just want to hear them forever.

His face comes to rest on my back, his breathing heavy as he comes down from the high, and I chuckle through the pain in my chest. I don't know why I'm feeling it, except suddenly I want to cry. I don't feel confused at all, but I feel defeated. Like I'll never be able to leave him even if he doesn't give me answers, and damn it.

I want them.

I need him to be my safe space, and he's not going to give me that as long as I don't know what the fuck is going on, how everything works around here. He doesn't trust me like I need him to. I see the darkness in him, the lies, the deceit. Something has changed in him since he left me in that basement. He used to be light, carefree, mine. Now he's all about me being his, yet letting Killian fuck me too. He's giving me whiplash. What about this society, this cult, makes all of this okay? Why the fuck is he treating me this way? I can't fucking do this anymore if he can't give in and trust me. If he wants to keep me in the dark forever.

Drav pulls out of me, going to the other side of the kitchen and wetting a rag, then cleaning me up with it gently. I don't want to love his gentleness with me, I want to hate it more than anything. But he can be so good to me. He treats me like I'm made of glass and maybe I am.

Not really.

"We need to talk." I tell him as he wipes himself now. "You're keeping secrets."

"I will always keep secrets, Firefly."

Something snaps inside of me, and I practically fly off the counter to get the knife beside me. I turn around quickly and press it to his throat hard enough to immediately draw blood. The way he hisses makes me smile so widely it hurts my cheeks.

Slice.

Do it.

He will never tell you the truth.

"Think again, baby boy." I continue with a grin. "You will tell me whatever the fuck I want to know if you don't want your sweet blood spilled on this fucking floor." I step up to him, licking the blood trailing down his bare chest. "Mmm, Draven. You're so *sweet*. Tell me the truth and I'll clean you up with my tongue. Pinky promise."

"Spill my blood, baby. I dare you."

I press the knife harder against his throat until I see a deeper cut, and he hisses. "I'm quite enjoying this, *baby*. Now fucking talk."

"It's loyalty to death," he replies angrily. "You wouldn't understand, but they saved me. I serve them now, they *saved* me from my prison and I have to repay them. Besides, I'm a Heathen now, part of *The Family*, and I don't have choices. They make them all for me, I'm their fucking puppet, Angel, and there's nothing I can do to stop them from pulling my strings."

I roll my eyes and keep the smile on my face, but it's my own strings that are close to snapping. I feel used by him, by this stupid hierarchy that I don't understand. He wants me to be his perfect girl, the docile one, the one who doesn't fucking ask any questions.

It's not you.

It's not me.

Damn right it's not.

"I know about your dad, you know," I snap. "I know he's a politician, I know that they put you in a position of *power* to serve their own agenda. Now what the fuck is *The Family?* I deserve to know that much." He doesn't ask me how I know about his dad, it's pretty obvious Killian was the one who told me.

Well, maybe he shouldn't have left you alone with him.

Drav sighs. "*The Family* is a hierarchy." I tilt my head to the side to urge him to talk more—trying to control myself and not snap at him that I know it's a hierarchy

—the knife still to his throat. It bobs and more blood trickles down. I don't ease up on it. "There are thirteen founding families, and our fathers make up The Fellowship, which is part of our society. The sons—*us*—are The Heathens."

I nod as if I understand, even though this is getting more confusing by the second. "And how many Heathens are there? What are soulmates?"

"There's six of us, and we're divided into pairs— that's what a soulmate is. We've grown up together, well at least they all did. I came in way later as you know, and they paired me up with Killian because they had odd numbers and he didn't have one. Soulmates are meant to have someone to confide in, to be your partner in crime. Sometimes...literally. We're supposed to have no secrets, and nothing to keep us apart. We're supposed to share everything, even wives if it's requested by the other."

"So all this time you were going to share me?" My outrage must show in my voice because his eyes widen, surely scared I'm about to go deeper with this trusty little knife.

"Fuck, no. You are the only thing I've kept from him, and he clearly doesn't like that. He wants to be in control, Angel. He's first in command of The Heathens."

"And you?"

"His right hand." He sighs. "Second in command. But he rules, just like *Dux*, our father."

"So let me get this straight. *The Family* is all of you.

But then what? What's the purpose? What do you control?"

"Government decisions," he replies slowly. "And other shit I don't want you to know about. It's endless and corrupt, and I don't want you involved."

I cackle. "Don't fucking push me, Draven. The knife might just *slip*." I shake my head, remembering the ritual. "Why the fuck do you have a brand on your chest? Why do *I* have one on my hand? What are you in charge of? And don't say the government."

That would not be the entire truth.

Drav looks guilty. "You'll hate me, and never want me to touch you again..."

"I won't." I raise my chin in defiance. "Now tell me the fucking truth."

"We have brands to show we're part of a...unit. A cohesive group that puts each other first. We are in charge of a lot of underground criminal activity. Human trafficking, organ trafficking...the black market. I could keep going."

"And if you're in charge, both of you, then who isn't?"

"The Vipers do our dirty work." He grabs my wrist, not pushing me away but also looking nervous. "But we're in charge of the operations...present too. We oversee everything they do. Approve it. Make it happen."

"So why weren't they part of the ritual?"

"Only the highest ranking Vipers are part of the inner circle. Yeah, they get some of the benefits we do, but not all of them. As far as the outer circle goes, well they do our dirty work. They take lead in the human trafficking," Draven's face is pained. His eyes glisten and he looks away momentarily before focusing them back on me. "They kidnap. They even kill for us in the most brutal ways."

I gasp and he grimaces.

"Every sick and fucked up thing you can imagine from gutting a man or raping an innocent." He continues, "I'm not proud of any of it, Angel, but I couldn't say no. I was initiated and thrown into the fire. If I were to defy The Fellowship...they would slice my stomach open and force feed me my own insides while laughing. There is no choice. Unless you pick death."

My head spins, making me dizzy. I'm part of this corrupt organization now, with no way out. Maybe I could run, hide somewhere they'll never find me. But where? How? I have no cash, no connections, no car. No knowledge of my surroundings. Not that it matters. I'll drive aimlessly if needed.

"Don't even get ideas to escape, Angel. I know you. I see it in your face, baby," he murmurs. "There's nowhere you can go that *The Family* won't find you, and I'll be at the head of the scavenger hunt. You'll never ever be away from me again. *Ever*."

My heart stops in my chest for a brief moment, only one. But he sees it and pushes the knife away. I push it into his stomach instead, then ask him, "What did you do for your initiation, Drav?" I think I'm going to throw up. I can't imagine him doing what I saw the other day. I can't think of him like that, with disgust. "What did you *do*?"

"I don't want to talk about that, Angel," he replies sadly. "But I'll tell you the ritual from the other day... that's not the worst thing we've done."

I tense and my hands begin to shake, but I asked for this right? I asked for his truths. Now I'm fucked because I'll never be able to unlearn this, and the more he talks, the more I don't want to be here. What kind of shit are they going to force me to do?

"You don't have to participate." It's as if he's reading my mind. "It's men only."

My body relaxes slightly, as if that makes anything better. It really doesn't but maybe I'll get to live in peace, in my own little bubble, and not have to think about all the shit he and Killian get into. I let the bloody knife down by my side and watch as the cut in his neck bleeds even more. It's not deep, but just deep enough that I know it will leave a scar. *My* scar. *Mine*.

I set the knife on the counter and lick his chest, feeling the blood coating my lips, then grab his face and bring it to mine. "I told you I'd lick you all better, baby." I purr, kissing him sweetly, chastely, just a peck. So unlike the way he fucked me, or even how I just had a knife to his throat. "Thank you for being honest." I tell him and mean it. "I don't want you to hide things from me."

"I will always hide something, Firefly." Tears well up in my eyes, because I don't know if I can deal with that. "There are things that make me a monster, a monster that isn't even worth you but will keep you all the same. There's situations...things that happen in our operations, the rituals, the dark shit we do...that I don't want you to know about. You'll never look me in the eye again if you know them, and I already told you—you're never leaving me again. I'm not a good guy anymore, my sins rule my life. The Fellowship and Killian rule *me*. As long as I live, I'll have to do their bidding. And I'll do what they say, but I won't give them an inch when it comes to us."

I think on that for a moment, wondering if Killian will fuck us over again and tear us apart. He will definitely try, I can sense that much, and I'm scared. I don't ever want to be without Drav.

"Just don't let him take me, Drav." I beg him. "*Don't*."

"Never." He promises. "You're my light in the darkness, Firefly." I breathe in deeply. "Without you, there's no light, remember?"

"I love you." I whisper.

He doesn't say it back, instead he kisses me like his life depends on it, stealing my breath and making my stomach swoop. I hope we're always like this.

Together.

But the moment is quickly over when there's a knock at the door, and Draven goes to open it. I follow closely behind and when he opens the door, there stands a man with a bouquet of black roses.

"For the lady." He says, and Drav takes it.

Slamming the door, he hands them to me and walks away, clearly pissed off. The moment is over. *Got it*.

I set them on the counter and look at them. No one's ever gotten me flowers, and Killian knows I was trapped in a basement for freaking ever. I know they're from him before I even look at the note. I turn the card attached to the flowers, my stomach dropping. He's doing this on purpose, to piss Draven off. I shouldn't like it, but it feels...sweet.

I'm coming for you, little demon.

-K.

A shiver runs down my spine and I walk away from the roses. Dreading the note, what it says. Now I know I won't be able to sleep at night, waiting for his arrival. Because he means it, and he will deliver on his word.

Until death do us part.

That's how long I'll be his, and now I know there's no escaping him. He probably will tear me and Draven apart with his bare hands.

And there's nothing we can do.

CHAPTER TEN

KILLIAN

T wo weeks.

That's how long it's been since I've talked to Angel. I don't know what's gotten into me, but I'm going fucking insane. I've been watching her, sending her roses every day. She hasn't even noticed me standing outside my house, following them around when he takes her out to show her around town. She really has been sheltered, and he has been taking her everywhere around Silent Grove. To restaurants, the mall, the movies. At this rate I won't even be able to take her somewhere new if I wanted to. I'll have to go out of town or something.

Why do I even care so fucking much?

The truth is, I've never felt this way before. Like I can't breathe properly. Every day that goes by I feel more desperate to know what she's doing, where she is, how often she gives *my* pussy to my brother. It's killing me, living quite literally next door and not being able to do anything about how much I want her. I guess I could if I wanted to, but for some fucked up reason I want her to actually want me, and maybe after I know for sure she'd stay, then I'll take her for my damn self. But right now she doesn't trust me, doesn't know me. I can't blame her for not wanting to give me a chance. All I've shown her is the lengths I'm willing to go to get what I want. She should be flattered, but instead she's fucking pissed. Maybe she really did want to marry Draven and I messed that up for them. Regardless, I don't give a fuck. She should've never come between us. We've always shared everything, and he didn't even tell me she was coming until I heard it from my father. After that I was determined to talk him into sharing, but he refused, saying she was off limits.

Nothing is off limits between us.

He fucking knows that.

We're soulmates, brothers, way more than that if I'm not mistaken. We're a lot, but estranged is not one of them. So now that he doesn't want anything to do with me, that he's giving me the cold shoulder, it's driving me fucking insane. I need to find a way to get him and Angel back to me, back to what happened two weeks ago. Both of them in my bed, but I'd settle for just Angel at this point. She's driving me up a fucking wall, goddamn insane over her.

Is it truly related to sex? I mean, she's the best pussy I've ever had, I'll be honest. It may have to do with the fact that she's basically a virgin, but I think it's way more than that. I just can't quite put my finger on it. Just *why* the fuck do I want her so bad? Is it because he does too? Do I just want everything he does? Is sharing everything with him that important to me? Or is it truly *her*?

Maybe I'm love drunk on her blood or something.

I feel bewitched, like she cast a spell on me that there's no way out of. We are bound by blood, by *The Family*, but it has to be more than that. I think one day I'll figure out what's wrong with me, just not anytime soon. But who cares? All that matters is that I do feel this way, and I have to have her. If I do, if she willingly lets me have her and doesn't put up a fight, if she even just pretends, then I'll be able to fuck her out of my system. I'll feel appeased, like she actually fucking wants me. Yeah, that's what I'm seeking from her, some reassurance that this is real between us. And it is, I know it is. She can't pretend it's not, she's not a good actress, after all she's not used to doing it. Angel may deny how she feels, but I feel it in my bones every time she looks at me. This connection we share, like fucking electricity sparking between us, a live wire. When she ran from me I felt this primal urge to fuck her until there was nothing left of her. I've never wanted someone so bad in my entire life. I've never felt this pure, unadulterated, blinding, black-out obsession before. It's ruling my life, taking over. Ruining it. Ruining *me*.

The fire sparks and crackles and pops, reminding me of her, and I tense with my Corona in my hand. I take a swig, swallowing it down with my feelings of inadequacy. Am I not good enough for her? Is that what this is about? Is Drav the good fucking boy in this dynamic? She likes that shit? I could be her good boy too, just not in the way she expects from me.

"Dude," Jagger says with wide blue eyes, annoyance in his voice. Well guess what? I'm more annoyed at the interruption of my thoughts. Even if they're fucking tragic. "Lighten up. It's just pussy."

"That pussy," I spit out, "belongs to my fucking *wife*. And now things are tense between Drav and I, and I don't know that they'll ever get better."

"Well maybe you shouldn't have taken her away from him." Asher interjects with a snigger. I want to gouge his pretty little green eyes out for it. It's none of their business whether I take something from Draven or not. He's my soulmate. *Mine*. "You ever think about that?"

"No." I chuckle, being honest. When I want something, I take it. I fucking get it. It's just my nature. I don't have time to be a pussified, submissive asshole. No, I'm the fucking alpha and Draven needs to understand that. I think he does, he just doesn't want to submit when it comes to her. It's a damn shame, we could be having so much fun together. "I wanted *them*, and he wanted her. So I took her." I shrug.

"So you never wanted her?" Asher asks me, his blond hair spilling over one eye, his other green one connecting with my own. "What kind of fucked up shit is this?"

"I wanted him to fucking share her with me!" I snap. "I wanted things to be as they always have been. But he didn't want that, no. And that only made me want her more. And now she's the only fucking thing I think about. Nothing else crosses my mind. I can't function like this, just waiting and holding my breath for another fucking glimpse of her."

"Dude, you're fucked." Says Jagger with a smirk on his lips. "But you said you wanted them? As in *both*?"

"You know how this shit works."

"Uh, no." Asher shakes his head at me with a laugh. "Jagger and I may be soulmates but we don't want to be together. You and Draven have always had your own thing, no matter how platonic it's been. We think it's been platonic anyway. Has it?"

"Yeah." I reply without hesitation, refusing to give them crumbs of my stolen moments with Draven. Tongues, lips, teeth...darkness. Bodies molding together, sweating, slick with pleasure. No, that's for me to keep buried deep in my dark, stained soul. "Platonic."

"But you want him?"

"Bro, he'd crawl over glass for Draven. Look at him!" Jagger chuckles, but it's not fucking funny how right he is.

"Oh, shit." Asher says as he looks behind me, and I tense. "Incoming."

"Great." I mutter under my breath.

I don't bother turning around to see who's there. I already know it's Draven, coming to hear all about the exchange we have to take care of. I'm the one who's organized everything, and I have to give the news. There's much to talk about, like how he's going to lead this operation: coke and weapons exchange. I know he hates it, but it's necessary. And I may or may not have assigned it to him on purpose so I could steal a moment or two with my little demon.

The air is suddenly thick as he sits next to me on the Adirondack chair, and my breath rushes out of my lungs when I see who drops onto his lap out of the corner of my eye.

Angel.

She's wearing a Mystic University hoodie that reaches almost to her knees, with no pants on, and a pair of high-top chucks. Her hair is messy and wavy, unkempt, and she has circles underneath her eyes. Yet she's still the prettiest girl I've ever seen. When she looks at Draven, a wide smile takes over her face, accentuating the sharp angle of her cheekbones. She turns her head forward to give me a view of the straight slope of her small nose, the bow of her top lip, her thick blonde lashes fanning over skin. It all hurts my fucking chest.

But what the fuck is she doing here? This is official business. She shouldn't be here, shouldn't know about our operations. Did he tell her everything? Did he beat me to it? That was my trust building exercise, just like I did back before we got married. He stole that from me, but it's only fair since I stole her. You can't have everything, Killian.

Chill the fuck out.

She chose *him*.

And according to the council meeting, it's fair game. But then again, all is fair in love and war. Right now, I don't know the difference when it comes to the three of us. Is this war? Is this war over love? But no, I don't love her. Am I hopelessly obsessed? Hell yes I am. Maybe it's war over obsession. I don't fucking know anymore.

I stare out into the pond, refusing to look at them, and pretend I'm looking at the most riveting sight in front of me even though the water is barely visible under the new moon and it's murky as fuck anyway. The nerve of Draven to bring her to my house without considering my feelings. Besides, this isn't a beer and chill session. We're here on *official* business.

And here he is rubbing her in my face.

"What is she doing here?" I ask through gritted teeth, because I won't start talking about everything until I either know she knows something, or she leaves my fucking house.

A silence descends upon us, and just as Draven opens his mouth to reply, Branden and Seth—the rest of The Heathens and soulmates—show up and sit across from us. They catch the vibe, but Branden—as always—tries to lighten up the atmosphere.

"Do you always need to hold our meetings in the middle of the fucking woods? It's giving Pine Pinnacle vibes." He smiles as if he enjoys what happens there—all our rituals, the fucking sacrifices, the blood drinking—and I know he does. He might look like a fucking saint among us, but I bet he's the most dark and twisted of us all. The *quiet* one. They're the ones to worry about. His brown eyes crinkle as he smiles, but it quickly smooths out when his eyes settle on Angel. He looks apprehensive—as he should be. A cold gust of wind blows over us and I see Angel shiver from the corner of my eye, though I focus on the way Branden's black hair blows with the wind, the way his strong nose scrunches and he sucks his full bottom lip into his mouth as he looks at my girl.

"It's peaceful here." I reply with a sigh, stretching my legs out in front of me, pretending I don't want to skin alive anyone and everyone who dares to look at Angel. "This is official business, Draven. She's gotta go."

"She's not going anywhere."

"What does she know?" I ask him with narrowed eyes, finally looking at him. His face tells me nothing, and the fucker has a good poker face, I'll give that to him. It makes me want to beat the shit out of him.

"Everything." Angel says with a shrug and all of us laugh.

Her face turns red with rage—almost like she wants to hurt me, stab me, *something*—and when my laughter finally dies down, I look her in the eyes and say, "I highly doubt that, baby girl. But I bet you know more than Draven is letting on, so I'll let you stay for the first part. The second part though? You'll get the fuck out of here if you know what's good for you." Amalia's disappearance is none of her fucking business. She's the daughter of my father's soulmate, and he's been disobeying his leaders. The Fellowship are still not the top motherfuckers around here. It seems like there's always someone above each society—it's never fucking ending. But if I had to guess...he's not following some kind of order and his daughter got taken to make a point. Do it, or she's dead. Yeah, that's probably the outcome.

"Careful, Kill." He points at his neck. "She's been feisty lately."

I look at the wound on his neck and Angel raises a brow at me. "Angel leaves for the second part." Is all I say, uncaring of the little fire flaring in her irises. I don't really care about how she may react.

Draven and I make eye contact at that, and he nods once. I don't have to say it for him to understand this is top fucking secret. And it is.

"Alright, Draven." I continue to hold his gaze, and feel hers hot on my face, but I don't stray my eyes from his. "There's a shipment of coke and guns. It's your turn to take this one."

Angel stiffens at my words, and I look down. Her hands have a death grip on the chair, her knuckles turning white, and I smirk. But her face is determined, her eyes hard, her lips set into a thin line. She's trying to be strong right now—or maybe she just is. Maybe she can handle this knowledge after all. Angel thinks she wants to know our business, so let her. Now she'll have to get a little colder, a little less sensitive if she wants to deal with this information. I was starting to think she'd be better off in the dark, just as Draven wanted her. Now, I'm not so sure. I want to give her the benefit of the doubt for the sake of seeing what she's capable of—what she can handle. It's a good thing she has no friends, because if she blabbed, even I couldn't save my poor little wife.

"We can talk about the details later." He replies, nodding once, and I roll my eyes.

This is why Angel shouldn't be here. She doesn't need to be listening in to half stories and then being kicked out. He doesn't want me to give details, except

I'm sick and tired of my second in command trying to tell me what to fucking do.

"No." I shake my head. "If you want her to stay she hears all of it." His arms wrap around Angel's waist protectively and heat rushes from my chest to my ears. I want to cut those fucking arms off. But Angel looks at me like she's waiting for me to continue, which she probably is, and I look at her when I say, "Draven, you will meet with Armando and Damien for the coke." They work for the cartel somewhere in San Antonio, Texas. "Camden," the first in command of the Vipers, "will meet you for the guns. You'll be in charge of this operation. It's your turn to organize it and oversee it. Seth did the last one, it's only fair."

"You want me to do the exchange with all of us together?" His face pales slightly, which makes me smile. I didn't take him for someone who'd be scared of a little exchange. He never has been before. Unless that's not what he's scared of. Maybe it's leaving her alone.

"Why not? Two birds with one stone, or whatever, right?"

"Isn't that a little...dangerous?"

"Damien and Camden do business all the time." I reply with a roll of my eyes, "They're not gonna fuck each other over. Damien is not the kind of guy you fuck with anyway, so Cam wouldn't dare."

"When?"

"Tomorrow night at eleven."

"That's a bit soon, don't you think?" Draven asks, running a hand down his face.

Now he's starting to annoy me. "Don't worry, I'll look after *our* girl."

Draven curses and I laugh, but it's not with humor. I hate him right now. I technically could meet with Damien and Camden, but I don't fucking want to. I'm going to use that time to pay my baby girl a visit, without interruptions. I won't have very long, but I've waited enough. And if he shows up before I leave? Even better. I kind of want him to know I'm not giving up. That there's nothing he can do about it either.

"The fuck you will." He growls, and Angel jumps.

"You seem a bit tense, Angel." I taunt. She doesn't even look at me. The entire time we've been here sitting next to each other she's looked at me only once, and it's bothering me, eating at me. It's like I don't exist, or I'm not worth her time. Well, she definitely isn't worth mine, but here I am, obsessed and shit. I hate it. "Someone get my *wife* a drink, she needs to relax."

"You do need to relax, baby." Draven murmurs and I tense, ready to snap his skinny fucking neck. "I'll be right back."

Draven gets up and walks toward the house—at least a three minute walk one way—and leaves her sitting next to me. The other guys don't even look at us, now chatting about the cartel and the guns and the coke. I have no interest in any of that shit. No, I'm worried about the girl sitting next to me who won't give me the time of day. I just want a little attention from her, and I'm going to get it one way or another.

"So you're not gonna talk to me now?" I ask her softly, keeping my voice low.

"Nope."

I chuckle, loving the chase and hating it all the same. "Aren't you curious about what's going on between us, little demon?" I look at her perfect profile. Straight, small nose. Pouty lips. High cheekbones. Long, blonde lashes. She's *perfect*. I've never had a thing for blondes, but this one? She's really doing it for me. "I know you feel it too."

Her breath whooshes out, and at this she looks at me, her face pink. "I don't know what you're talking about."

"Come on, baby girl. Stop lying to yourself. You think about me when he's sleeping, you fucking want me too." She searches my eyes as if she's looking for truths in them. Well she's in luck, I'm giving them all away. "How many times has he made you come and I was the one on your mind?"

She looks away, saying with finality, "None."

I reach out to touch her hand, reaching over my seat, leaning into her. A shock goes through me when our skin meets, and her head snaps to the side, her eyes meeting mine. "Don't you miss me on top of you?" I whisper, getting closer until my mouth is against the shell of her ear. My lips brush against her soft skin and she shivers. "Don't you wish I could show you what I can offer you? And it's not just sex." I lick the shell of her ear and then bite her earlobe. Her teeth clamp down on her bottom lip and my cock grows painfully, restrained by my jeans. "I'd give you everything. Every part of me. I'd give you what he won't."

"Oh?" She turns her head and looks at me, her lips brushing against mine, her forehead pressed to my own. "And what's that?"

Our breaths mingle, our lips brush, our eyes stare into each other's. "All of my truths."

She's quiet for a beat, looking at my lips then back up to my eyes. Then she pulls away, shoving my hand off her chair. "I don't think you know how to tell the truth."

"You don't know me at all. Draven is the one you need to worry about." I know how to take a hint, rejection even, and return to my chair. "You'd do well to remember that."

Draven comes back with a drink in his hand and a joint between his fingers, and Angel gets up from the chair to return to her place on his lap. "Give me." She tells him with a smile that I wish was directed at me. Heat rushes through my body at his smirk, the one that says he knows where this is going later. Well, not if I have anything to fucking do with it. "I want some."

"Angel." He shakes his head, white blond hair spilling over his forehead just as my own does sometimes. I just want to run my fingers through it, yank it back when I'm fucking him. My blood heats as I look at him, and when we make eye contact he slightly flinches. I know he can see it in my eyes, in my face—my thoughts. The way I want to take him here right in front of everyone without a care in the world. He looks away from me, looks at her, and my fists clench. "You don't even know how to smoke this."

"So teach me."

"You shouldn't do this." She shouldn't. At least he has some common fucking sense. Well, I take that back now, because he's putting the joint between her lips. "Okay, don't bite it, now. Suck on it and inhale."

She does.

Except it's like she takes three hits with the way she keeps inhaling deeply.

"Stop, stop, baby." He chuckles. "Now let it all out."

Angel begins to cough violently, the smoke escaping through her nose and lips, and she turns red as she doubles over. I roll my eyes at his poor instructions, but I keep my mouth shut for once. He hands her the shot glass in his hand and she drinks it, sputtering a bit when she's done. The guys all laugh at her, and a smile quirks up my lips, but again I stay quiet. Maybe this will serve me later. She looks more relaxed, more pliable. Maybe I can get her alone soon.

"Time for official business." I announce, looking at Drav pointedly, hinting to get her the fuck out of here. "Men *only*." I clarify, just in case his dumbass isn't getting the hint.

Angel doesn't even look at me as she gets up and starts walking away, and a prickle of anger makes my hands itch as if there's ants biting them. I don't want to kick her out, but this really is official business. There's nothing about this she needs to be hearing. But the way she gives me her back without a glance at me makes me want to put her over my knee and spank her ass raw.

"I'll walk you in," Draven offers. "You've never been in this house."

"I'll figure it out," she replies, swaying on her feet. Obviously the marijuana was going to hit her hard considering the long hit she took and it being her first time. He's fucking stupid for letting her have some. Maybe she'll get lost on the way in and drown in the pond instead. Sure as fuck would solve all my problems if she was out of my life. No one to obsess over. "It's just a house."

Draven stays in his seat as she walks away, and when I see she's going the right way and not into the pond I'm momentarily disappointed. I shake my head, trying to get my head in the game, and look at the boys.

"Amalia has disappeared." Seth and I look at each other because it's his sister. "Someone hasn't been following orders, and I'd bet anything it's Samuel." Seth's father and my own father's soulmate. Second in command. Now the thing we need to know is what orders he hasn't been following, why his daughter has been taken, and where they're hiding her.

Seth's eyes widen. "I don't have any information, if that's what you're implying. It's not like my father runs shit by me, Kill."

"*Dux* wants us to figure out why she's missing, and where she is."

Asher looks at me for a moment with a frown on his face, "Why would anyone want Amalia Rothschild?"

"Why would anyone not?" I scoff, incredulous. Have they learned nothing? "She's clearly leverage. Samuel did something, and they're using her against him. Now I'm assuming they don't want money for her, or she'd be home already, so I have to figure out why she's gone, who took her, and why. My father doesn't know exactly what's going on," Now I direct my gaze to Seth. "And you will shut the fuck up if you know what's good for you."

"What happens with The Heathens is *our* fucking business, no one else's," Seth says as he leans back in his chair and stretches out his legs in a nonchalant and relaxed gesture that I know is fake as fuck. His sister is missing and he's now keeping secrets from his father, who is above us. He's not fooling anyone. "You have nothing to worry about."

Except I do.

I have plenty to worry about, because if he has even the slightest slipup, if he even acts differently toward his dad, he will make him suspicious. "Seth, as far as you're concerned...you don't know anything. You didn't hear this. Do you understand?" I ask through gritted teeth. "Or it's your life on the line. Disobedience is not tolerated."

"We live by the rules, we die by the rules." He all but chants, lighting a joint.

"Good." I nod, "You fucking keep that in mind."

The guys change the subject at that, trying to make light of the situation. All except Seth. It's his sister, and I know he can't make light of it. They're basically twins, being born nine months apart. I don't blame him for being distressed, but he needs to keep it together so this can work.

We have to get this done or my father will skin me alive.

His tasks are *never* to be taken lightly.

"I gotta piss." I mutter, getting up from my chair and walking toward my house before anyone can object, not that they would. I'm mostly thinking of Draven.

I smirk as I get closer to the house, intent on finding my little demon. It's eerily quiet when I walk in, and I look around the living room and kitchen first but there's no one there. She's probably in the bathroom, but I don't give a damn. I'm busting through the door if that's what it takes to talk to her.

Making my way up the stairs, I check the bathroom to find it empty. *Interesting.* I go room by room, opening doors to see if she's in there, but come up empty. Where are you?

"Where are you, little demon?" I yell out, and immediately hear shuffling coming from the only open door left—my room.

There's more shuffling, or rustling—maybe my sheets, but she doesn't reply. I push the door open further to find her staring up at the ceiling, her legs dangling off the bed, her long hoodie hiked up on her thighs, revealing lacy underwear I'm sure Drav bought her.

For himself.

Either way, my dick gets hard in my pants because I'm fucking human, no matter how pissed off that makes me. She doesn't even look at me when I walk toward her, the only indication she knows I'm here is her speeding breaths, the heaving of her chest.

I get between her legs, nudging them with my knees, and lean over her until she has to meet my eyes. "You hiding from me, baby girl?"

"Always," she whispers.

Heat rushes through me, I don't know what it's attributed to, but I don't like it. Somehow it feels less like anger and more like rejection, and that bothers me. That she's fucking rejecting me.

"Don't you know you can't escape me?"

"One day I will."

I chuckle at that lie. She will never, *ever*, be able to. "No you won't."

"What do you want, Killian?" She snaps. "Why do you keep coming to me?"

"You suck my soul out, little demon." I breathe, getting on my knees for her, looking at her underwear from an angle. "I just can't help myself. Something is pulling me toward you."

"You don't have a soul."

We both smile at that, and I trail my fingers up her legs. "Don't I?" She sucks in a sharp breath. "Maybe I need spiritual healing then, what do you think?"

"I—" My nose comes to her underwear and I inhale deeply, making her close her legs around my head. "You're fucking crazy."

"For you, yes." I can't even deny it. I am *insane* for her. "Let me in, Angel. Give me a chance."

I lick over her panties, her legs spreading for me as far as they'll go, and I lick her again. Fuck, all I want is for her clit to be between my lips, I need to taste her, not her fucking underwear. So I do just that, shoving her underwear to the side, and sealing my mouth against her clit. I lick her, twirling my tongue against her glistening pussy, and she moans long and low.

"God, *Killian*." She moans again. "That feels so good."

I know it's the weed talking, making her even more sensitive, but I don't even care. I can't find myself giving a fuck right now as she gushes all over my chin. I moan like she's the one sucking me off, and she grips my hair hard.

Angel swivels her hips, riding my face, and I groan at how wet she is, the sweet taste of her. But suddenly she stops, catching her breath. "I'm with Draven, and nothing will change that."

My stomach drops as she pushes me away, and my heart somersaults when the door creeps open. "Please, Angel." I whisper, basically begging.

I don't want to do it, but I'll fucking take her. I'll keep her away from him even if she's not willing.

"What," Draven's low voice is at my ear, sending shivers down my spine, "the fuck is going on?"

"Hmm?" I ask as I let her underwear fall back in place, her wetness dripping down my chin. I turn toward him and lick my bottom lip, letting him witness the glistening evidence of her arousal. "Do you want a taste, baby?"

"I don't want a fucking taste, Kill." He shakes his head, though he still looks at my lips and gets on his knees next to me. His blue eyes dilate, black swallowing blue. "We're getting out of here."

"That's too bad." I whisper for his ears only. "Here I

was wanting a repeat, but maybe I'd fuck you instead. Wouldn't you like that, Drav? To be filled up by my cock?"

"Shut the fuck up, Kill." His chest heaves, and I know he wants me. He always has, always will. I don't give a damn what he says or how he pretends not to. "Don't come near my girl again."

"It's a shame." I get closer, my lips against his. "It's a shame you don't want me, because that was some damn good dick."

Getting up, I back away from them, letting him help her get on her feet. They leave quickly, not even sparing a glance back, just like they did when they fucked me last. It kind of hurts, I won't lie, and I think my ego is taking a big hit. I don't care anymore about what I have to do to have them, I'm going to fucking go through with it.

Even if I ruin everything between Draven and me.

CHAPTER ELEVEN

ANGEL

There's a heated pool in the backyard, and I can't believe I'm here in Draven's house, in the middle of the night as I wait for him to get back from the job. I've never been so relaxed in my entire life, and when I was trapped in that basement, lonely and sad I'd think of nights like these. I just never thought I'd live them. I always imagined I'd be there for the rest of my miserable life.

It's no secret this life is a different type of prison, but a prison, nonetheless. I'm not hurting or caged in this house, I have a driver when I want it and I can get out, but I still know no one except for The Heathens, and no other girls have come around. I don't even know if there are any. Do Jagger, Asher, Branden, and Seth have girlfriends? Or are they casual type of men? They're older, in their mid-twenties, just like Killian. Draven is the youngest out of them all at twenty-two years old, closer to my age. As far as I'm aware, they're either all single or might have girlfriends, but none are married. Draven has been slowly filling me in on the lives of everyone around me, like where Killian's mom is: nowhere to be found. She abandoned him when he was little, left with some other man and moved to Europe somewhere. I'm honestly surprised she isn't dead. Or she is and he doesn't know. It's possible his father was the one who did it, after *Cinis* I know what type of people they are, what they're capable of. I can't be stupid and try to escape, I know they wouldn't hesitate to kill me, or worse.

It's a cold day in Virginia with it being mid-November, but it still doesn't stop me from sitting at the edge of the pool and dipping my legs in. I'm considering getting in, tank top and shorts and all, when I hear a rustling of clothes behind me.

God, don't do this to me right now.

Someone's breath caresses my right ear, and I close my eyes, my body tense. I know who it is before he speaks, his vanilla and leather scent filling my nostrils. Why did Drav have to go on business? Why did he leave me alone? And then it hits me, it's because Killian planned this all along.

"Hello, wife." He says softly against my ear, making me shiver. He sits behind me, his dick against my ass, and my air rushes out. "Did you miss me, baby girl?"

I gasp, not even thinking, and jump into the pool, rushing toward the damn steps on the other side. It's a miracle I can reach, because I don't know how to swim —at least I can't remember how. But when I look back he's still sitting there, not even bothering to come after me. He doesn't care about the cold as he sits at the edge of the pool wearing only shorts and no shirt on. His sculpted shoulders flex when he moves his hands to the edge of the pool, gripping it, and a knowing simper on his face. I can't stop looking at him...he's beautiful with his black floppy hair that falls over his sapphire blue eyes, his kissable lips, and a smile to die for. My pelvis heats up and butterflies take flight in my stomach when he grins at me, then takes his bottom lip between his teeth. He's indecent, he shouldn't be real, and I just want him to disappear from my sight so I don't do anything stupid.

I try to walk faster as I tread through the water, and when I reach the steps, I practically run up them and past the pool area. What the hell is it with these men wanting to live in the middle of the woods? It doesn't matter though, because I run toward them.

"You know what running after you does to me, little demon." He calls out, his voice husky. "I'd advise you to stop unless you want your face in the dirt again."

I stop in my tracks, not wanting to taunt him, but kind of curious all the same. Will it feel as good as it did that first night? Will he fuck my ass again, or my pussy this time? I want to find out, damn it, I really do. But that would be a betrayal to Drav, right? Or would it? I am *married* to this man. *Bound* in goddamned *blood*.

The confusion is killing me, but I can't do this, go down without a fight.

I hear footsteps behind me, and Killian comes around to face me, his face smug, eyes dark without the light shining against them. "You can't run from me, Angel. I'll always catch you." He shrugs nonchalantly, "Now come with me before I make you."

"Where?"

"*Home.*"

I laugh at that, "Hell no." His eyes narrow at me and I smile. I'm not going anywhere with him, he's freaking delusional and insane. "*This* is my home."

"The fuck it is."

"Killian." I put my hand up to stop him. "Please, don't."

Killian grins at that, "You scared?" I take a step back, looking back toward the pool. Maybe if I run fast enough I can get in the house and lock him out. "You should be."

Not bothering with an answer, I pivot and run toward the pool, trying to dodge it and go for the sliding glass doors right behind it. Except he's faster than me and catches up easily, grabbing my hair and yanking me toward him until my back meets his heaving chest. But I don't think it's from exertion like me, I think it's because he's fucking pissed or excited. Or both.

I yelp from the pain, feeling strands give way, but he doesn't even care as he pulls me toward the steps of the pool. I fight him, bucking my body and slapping behind me. My hand connects with his face and he chuckles.

"Harder, Angel." He grunts. "Hit me harder."

He's so fucking toxic. Why would he even want that? With every moment that passes I'm more convinced that he's utterly unhinged. For some twisted reason he lets go of my hair and allows me to turn around, and I take the opportunity to slap him as hard as I can across the face. Killian's head whips to the side, making me smile, and he grins, a little bead of blood on his lip. Barely there. Almost nonexistent unless you're up close.

"Is that all you got, little demon?" He whispers, turning his face to look at me, his blue eyes dilating and constricting over and over as he looks at me. "You don't want to hurt me then?"

Heat bubbles up in my veins as if someone has turned up the temperature to my anger and brought it to a boil. Impulsively, I get up on my tip toes and wrap my hands around his neck, digging in deep with my fingernails. His face is placid, though quickly turning red, and the grin he gives me makes my knees weak. Why does he have to be so beautiful? Why do I have to feel this way?

"You're making me crazy, *devil*." I say through gritted teeth, and his eyes sparkle as he turns a deeper shade of red, leaving his hands by his sides. I watch a little trail of blood run over my fingernail and I get the sudden urge to lick it and him. "I don't like it."

His hands wrap around my wrists and tug my hands off him, more like pry, and my nails dig in deeper. His skin is beneath them. I can see how he has my marks all over him, his skin raw. When he finally pries me off, I run them down his chest and abs lightly, making him jump, and I grin when I see the devil tattoo above the waistband of his shorts. My eyes linger on it, remembering what it looks like without clothes on, and I feel my ears heat up.

Killian takes a step back until he's a bit further in the pool, and he grabs my hair and twists it around his fist, shifting his fingers to grip my nape. I whimper when he tightens his grip and he brings his face close to mine. I can smell the hint of mint on his breath. Is he always this alluring? He's fucking unreal. The way his black hair is always falling over his eyes and he has to push it out of the way. His eyes a deep blue I could get lost in, his muscles always flexing under his clothes. His pouty lips begging to be kissed, so full and perfect. I. Want. Him. Yet I also don't.

I look away from him as much as my eyes will allow, and he doesn't like that. But he doesn't like a lot of things I do, so he can get over it. He bends down further until his lips are against mine, then bites my bottom one until I taste blood in my mouth. He's always so aggressive, so unlike the gentler nature of Draven. I love it, and I know I shouldn't.

Killian doesn't let go of my lip, instead sucking it into his mouth and soothing it with his tongue. I moan at the act, and his fingers tighten in my hair impossibly. I have to squeeze my thighs together to try to stop my clit from pulsing, but goddamn it's impossible. Even if I'll never admit this to him, I want my cheek pressed against those steps while he fucks me from behind. I'd let him drown me at this point.

My hands come to his face to try to pry him off, but with his free hand he pulls me toward him even closer, until our bodies are plastered against each other. He's not even on a step at all, he's fully in the water, although he's so tall it reaches the top of his thighs, unlike me.

"I know you want me, Angel." He says as he pulls away, and my chest heaves with my restraint as I try not to kiss him again. My hands fall to my side. "Let me ask you something."

"Yeah?"

"Have you ever sucked cock before?"

I laugh at that, low and throaty. "No. And I don't plan on starting tonight."

Killian smiles as if amused, a tilt to his lips that I need to look away from but can't. His white, straight teeth sparkle in the near darkness when his smile grows, and I realize it's because of how I can't stop staring at him. "I think since you're leaving with me, you might as well."

A shiver runs down my spine at his words, and I know he's not playing around. Maybe this is it, him enforcing our marriage, and grief hits me hard at the thought of not being with Draven anymore. My eyes well up with tears.

"Don't be sad, little demon." He tuts. "You won't miss him for long, I promise."

"It'll always be *him*, Kill." I taunt, wanting him to show me his crazy even though I mean it. I will never be over Drav or stop missing him. I shrug. "I'll never choose you."

"Shut the fuck up." He pulls my arm a little to the side, and I groan at the pain. "Not the right answer."

"What is the right answer then?"

"There isn't one." I just bet there isn't. I don't understand why he's so obsessed with me all of a sudden. He doesn't even know me. *The same way I am obsessed with him.* Fuck. "Now get on your fucking knees, little demon."

Killian doesn't wait for me to comply, instead he grabs me by the shoulders and pushes me down onto my knees, the water barely below my chin. He pushes his shorts down one handed and his cock bobs up toward my forehead, the water reaching part of his shaft.

"Don't worry, I'll tell you exactly what to do." My stomach flips as he grabs his cock and slaps my cheek with it. "Open that mouth, baby girl. From now on, I'm the only one you'll do this with. I'm the only God you'll know, and you'll fucking worship me just like you're about to do right now."

"I fucking hate you." Heat rushes through my body as his hand comes to the top of my head and he shoves me underwater. Then he yanks me by my hair and pulls me back up.

"Say that with a mouthful of my cock, then."

I open my mouth then, mostly because if I don't he'll probably drown me. At least that's what I keep telling myself. I reach up tentatively and touch him, and his cock jumps at the contact when I grip him and start to move my hand up and down. He moans and my stomach flips once more, butterflies fighting to the death in it.

"Lick it." He commands. "Get it all wet for you. Then open your mouth and let me in."

I lick him from shaft to tip, my tongue going over each individual piercing, trying to wet him with my saliva, then open my mouth.

"Tongue out baby girl, and don't fucking scrape me with your teeth."

With my tongue out, I direct him to my mouth. He

smells like *him*. So fucking good, and when I take him a little deeper, he shoves my head down until it's under-water again with his cock in my mouth. I gag, coming up for air.

"Oh, God." He groans. "So fucking good for me already. Now suck. Hollow your cheeks and suck my cock." I do, I hollow my cheeks and suck him, bobbing my head up and down. His cold piercings rub against my tongue lightly, and I shiver when he puts his hand above my head again. "Breathe in through your nose slowly, and when I push you down, you keep going. Don't pull away."

I grab his thighs and dig my fingernails into his skin, but I don't pull away, and when he pushes my head underwater, I don't resist. I keep bobbing my head up and down, pleasuring him, and his moans crescendo the faster I go. I'm out of breath, my lungs burning, and I pull up to breathe but he pushes me back down. My chest begins to hurt, my head begins to spin, and I dig my fingernails deeper even as I moan through it, loving to be used.

"You're such a whore for me, Angel." He groans and I hear it as I bob my head back up, breathing in through my nose quickly when I finally get the chance, "My dirty whore."

I moan again.

"Just like that, Angel. You're doing so fucking good."

Killian clamps a hand behind my head and fucks my mouth, increasing his pace so quickly I can't catch my breath, my head underwater for most of it. I try to bob my head, but it's useless, I have no rhythm with the way he's pounding into me, his piercings scraping my tongue. With a few more thrusts of his hips, I feel his cock twitch in my mouth, then he's coming, but he pulls out of me before I can get any more of him in my mouth. His cum gets on my belly as he grabs me by the throat and pulls me up, preventing me from swallowing.

"Spit in my mouth, baby girl."

He pulls me by my throat toward his lips and opens his mouth for me. I gather saliva and his cum and spit it slowly into his mouth, moaning when he does too. Fuck, he's so dirty. Draven would *never*.

Killian makes me feel things I shouldn't, but isn't that everything forbidden?

My throat hurts around his grip and I know I'll have bruises later. My lungs burn too, and my body feels fucking exhausted. I claw at his arms and he releases my throat slightly as I gulp in air, letting me take a step back.

"You've ruined me, Angel." He steps up to me and kisses me softly, sucking on my top lip, and me sucking on his bottom one. "Fuck. I don't know how to breathe without you anymore. Don't make me force you. Just come with me, *please*."

"Why?"

"You're in danger."

I scoff when he lets go of me. Fucking finally. "I don't believe you."

"I told you I wasn't going to let you go. You're all fucking *mine*." His nostrils flare as he says that, his eyes looking into mine with an intensity that makes me uncomfortable. "But I wouldn't do this to you unless there was a good reason for it. And there is, you're in danger. I can't explain why, not now. But you need to come with me."

"You need to *leave*." I tell him, my voice low and serious and cold. So unlike what we just did. What I did to him. "Draven is coming home soon—"

"I don't care, Angel." He says coldly, exactly like me. "You're coming with *me*."

"Does he know?" Fear curls my insides at the thought of Draven looking for me, losing me all over again. "That you're taking me?"

"He does." Killian nods once.

Kill grips me by the arm and drags me toward the house, stopping next to a small table with a syringe on it. I fight him, punching and dragging my feet, trying to get loose.

"What the fuck are you doing?"

"I'll take you by force, Angel." He sneers, and I've never seen him pissed off but I imagine it's this. "And The Fellowship won't stop me because you're my fucking wife!" He growls.

I don't resist anymore, my body tired.

"This is bigger than us." He says softly, nothing like the man he was just seconds ago. "I just want to keep you safe, Angel."

"Okay." I nod quickly. "Fine."

"Do you trust me?"

I shake my head and he laughs, grabbing the syringe from the table beside us. "Fuck. No."

"You'll be okay." Killian promises, kissing my cheek

softly, then he sticks the needle in my shoulder gently. "That's all I want for you, baby girl."

"Just do it." I close my eyes, "But I'll never forgive you."

"Yes, you will." He nods as he pushes the plunger all the way down. It's thick, and my arm hurts as the liquid goes in. I groan and he looks at me with a sympathy that makes me want to claw his eyes out. "Because I'll tell you everything when I can. Until then, I'll keep you safe."

"Kill—" I groan, my body going limp within a few seconds, and he catches me easily. What the fuck did he give me? But I don't have much time to think about it as the edges of my vision begin to blur. "*Killian.*"

Then my world spins on its axis and everything goes black.

To be continued...

AFTERWORD

This series is going to be a journey, one I hope you stick around for. These characters had a mind of their own the entire time I was writing them, and they still live rent-free in my head. Needless to say, they're all a little unhinged, just the way I like them. When I came up with the idea of this novella, I never intended for it to become MMF. But hey, I'm not one to complain, so just like everything related to Angel, Killian, and Draven I took it in stride. Thank you for giving this novella a chance, as well as myself. If you're not new here, thank you for sticking around.

So much love for you,
Shae Ruby

WHAT'S NEXT?

Thank you from the bottom of my heart for reading
Unhallowed! Please don't forget to review if you enjoyed
the book. Reviews are so important to indie authors
like me. I am forever grateful for your support!
If you'd like to be part of the community and talk about
the series, join the Facebook Group,
Ruby's Darklings.

STALK ME

My website is **authorshaeruby.com**
Sign up for my newsletter at
authorshaeruby.com/newsletter
Follow me on Facebook at
Facebook.com/authorshaeruby
Join my Reader Group at
Facebook.com/groups/rubysdarkling

ACKNOWLEDGMENTS

Unhallowed was written in a lust frenzy. It is everything I did not know I needed, and everything I wanted it to be. This series feels like the beginning of something incredible, different, and exciting. I hope that after getting a taste of it, you're dying to come back for more. More of **Killian**, too. That man just does things to me. I've definitely been nervous to release this novella. Mostly because it's the first time I've written something not related to The Broken Series. It feels like a very vulnerable moment for me, so thank you for sharing it with me. **Here's to new beginnings.** And thank *YOU.* Thank you for being here, giving me a chance, picking up this novella and giving me your time. Thank you for holding space for me.

To my husband, Conner, as always you are my rock. None of this would be possible without you. Thank you for always holding my head above water, the encourage-ment, and the support. I couldn't do this without you by my side. I love you endlessly.

To my mother, thank you so much for all the phone

calls, putting up with my ramblings, and listening even when you don't know what I'm talking about. But mostly, thank you for being here for me. I love you.

To C.L. Menegon, you my girl, are someone so special in my life it's hard to put into words. Your friendship means the world to me. Forever and ever. I love you so much.

To my amazing alpha and beta readers: Jay and Danielle, I couldn't have done this without you. Jay, thank you for always embarking on whatever wild ride I take you in. You're always down to read whatever new and shiny thing I throw at you, and it means everything to me. The way you always hold space for me and let me vulnerable is something I will never take for granted. Danielle, you've always been a freaking cheerleader for me and I'm always on the edge of my seat for your commentary. You're hilarious, my girl. I love you both!

To my Street Team and TikTok team, you guys are AMAZING!! Thank you for all your help. My marketing would be terrible without you guys (we can laugh about this). No, but seriously. You're ALL incredible and I am so grateful. Here's to many more books together!! I love you!

I also want to thank my team:

Angie from Lunar Rose Editing Services, I will never tire of telling you that I could not have done this without you, because it's the truth. Thank you for your partnership and friendship. And thank you for always holding space for me.

Quirky Circe, your creativity knows no bounds.

Thank you so much for always being open to my ideas, and for creating the beautiful work that you do.

Lastly, I want to thank my social media followers both on Instagram and TikTok, my Facebook page, and my Readers Group. None of this would be possible without you spreading the word about my book!

All of you mean everything to me.

With love,
Shae Ruby

ABOUT SHAE RUBY

**Author of dark romance & toxic love.
Sometimes diverse.**
Shae Ruby spends her time writing books
that make you *feel*.
When not writing you can find her spending time
outdoors or planning her next trip.
Music is her love language, as you can probably
tell by her playlists.

Shae Ruby is represented by Beck Literary Agency.
For all subsidiary rights, please contact Josi Beck:
jlbeck@beckromancebooks.com

ALSO BY SHAE RUBY

The Broken Series:

Shattered Hearts (Book 1)

Battered Souls (Book 2)

Tattered Bodies (Book 3)

The Tainted:

Bloody Tainted Lies (Book 1)

Printed in Great Britain
by Amazon

38414382R00119